Adda Leah Davis

A FATAL WEB OF DECEIT

Book Two of The Untangling Tale

ADDA LEAH DAVIS

abbott press

Abbott Press books may be ordered through booksellers or by contacting:

Abbott Press
1663 Liberty Drive
Bloomington, IN 47403
www.abbottpress.com
Phone: 1-866-697-5310

ISBN: 978-1-4582-1753-0 (sc)
ISBN: 978-1-4582-1755-4 (hc)
ISBN: 978-1-4582-1754-7 (e)

Library of Congress Control Number: 2014914279

Printed in the United States of America.

Abbott Press rev. date: 09/04/2014

DEDICATION

THIS BOOK IS DEDICATED TO ALL the wonderful, caring people, who have papered my life with their wisdom, understanding, caring and love. Every thought I have and every image I see is of some endearing person who used all their knowledge to help me build a strong outpost. Once this outpost was in place they knew that whatever storm or tempest came, I would have the knowledge to weather the storm and evolve as a better person. I thank God that each person was a part of my house of life.

Coming from a Scotch/Irish heritage made me independent as to carrying my own weight, but it also gave me love to help those who were unable to do things for themselves. My grandfather taught me to read from the New Testament and I often smile and say, "Thank you Grandpa."

By the age of ten I had read that entire book and knew most of the Bible stories which taught many, many lessons. So, with that in mind I think it would be fair to say that my writing is dedicated to our precious Lord.

ACKNOWLEDGEMENTS

THE 121ST PSALM SAYS: I WILL lift mine eyes unto the hills from whence cometh my help. My help cometh from the Lord…. And I find myself turning to the hills more and more in these troubling times. I often wonder how those who do not know the Lord can survive without His love to bear them up.

I wish to thank all my friends and fans who have encouraged me and helped me in many ways while writing this book. A writer needs encouragement and all of you have given me that in abundance.

My friend and editor, Rachel Riggsby, undoubtedly has the patience of Job because of her ability to be calm and gentle while telling me what needs to be changed. Thanks so very much Rachel.

I wish to thank the Bradshaw Library and especially Iris Ann Shelton and Brenda Baker who never fail to give me a call when a new book comes out. They and the Friends of the Library group make me feel like they've rolled out the red carpet for a grand opening. Thanks to each of you who come out to hear me talk and buy my book also.

My friends at the Appalachian Arts Center, the Reminiscent Writers Class, McFarlane Drug Company, Family Drug Company, and Tamarack in Beckley, West Virginia have all been helpful and supportive of all my writing. Thanks to all of you.

My dear brothers and sisters in the Lord in both the Elkhorn Association and the Three Forks of Powell's River Association have been the anchors that care for me and give me a home among them. I pray that our God bless each member in whatever they need for health, love, and peace in their lives.

Thanks to my husband, Unice for his help, especially this past year, in taking me places to do book signings. Also my beloved grandson, Jonathan who helps me prepare for a signing and loads the car before I leave and calls to check on me through the day. I thank God for the gift of Jonathan in my life.

SUCCESS IS A FICKLE LOVER

Success is a fickle lover,
casting lures far and wide
painting dreams of distant pinnacles
and lofty peaks, to flaunt one's pride.

Success is a devious lover
whose spangled lures sometimes enchant
by sprinkling gold along a pathway
and bewitched travelers have no complaint.

Success is a treacherous lover
extolling precipices yet unseen
and enthusing on the glorious pleasures
of fame and fortune there to glean.

Success can be a fatal lover
to all of those not faint of heart
who get ensnared in success's tendrils
and find their lives are torn apart.

"Nearly all men can stand adversity, but if you want to test a man's character give him power."
Abraham Lincoln

CHAPTER 1

HANNAH HORNE LARKIN HADN'T COMPLETELY RECOVERED from her recent stay in the hospital when her husband was found dead on her living room floor. The shock was devastating and she hadn't yet adjusted to that grief. Now, two days later, the police had arrested her son as a suspect in his father's murder. Without the help of God and Sarah Preston, a widow who was her best friend and neighbor, Hannah felt she couldn't have survived.

Hannah watched in a benumbed stupor as the patrol car pulled away from her front door with her son in the backseat. At the corner of Pike Lane the vehicle was lost from sight, but Hannah still stood stiffly watching with her jaws clenched. She stood a moment longer before turning from the door casing against which she had been bracing herself.

"God please, please help me," she begged silently as she sank into the first available chair and dropped her head into her hands.

"Don't give up, Hannah. You'll have to fight, but you don't have to do it alone. You just stand right up, grit your teeth and decide to win. God will always help you." Sarah cheered as she took a chair across from her friend.

At those words, Hannah, in a burst of emotion, pushed herself to her feet, again feeling strong. She stood with a martial gleam in her eyes, but then dropped to the floor in a senseless heap, banging her head in the process.

"Hannah! Oh my God!" Sarah fell to her knees beside the prostrate body of this young friend that she loved like a daughter.

Feeling her pulse, Sarah mumbled, "Thank God, she's alive!" She jumped to her feet and ran to the kitchen, returning with a wet wash cloth. When the cold water hit Hannah's face, she moaned and opened her eyes.

Sarah waited, not knowing what to expect. When Hannah lay staring at her, she became uneasy. "Hannah, do you know me? This is Sarah."

Hannah lifted her hand and touched Sarah's arm. "I know you're Sarah, but I don't know why I'm lying in the floor or why you're staring at me."

Sarah smiled. "Let's get you up and I'll tell you. I don't like to look down on people."

Hannah grinned and sat up, shaking her head. "I feel fuzzy-headed."

Sarah grasped her hands and pulled her onto her feet. Hannah stood still for a moment and then returned to her chair.

"No wonder you feel 'fuzzy-headed.' You hit that floor hard enough to make you fuzzy-headed or worse."

Hannah closed her eyes momentarily, then again tried to focus on Sarah. She could see, but this time from wild, fright-filled eyes. "It's that awful-tasting medicine I was given when Bill died. It's making me feel awful. I have to help Freddie, and I can't do that if I can't stay on my feet. I'm going to throw it away, Sarah."

"I wouldn't do that, Hannah. You've just had another bad shock."

"Shock! You're right there. Every time I come to the top of the stairs I see Bill all crumpled up at the bottom, but that's nothing like Freddie's look when that sergeant accused him of murdering his daddy. I don't know what to do right now, but I know I have to do something."

"Well, you can't do it now, so come and drink some tea, rest a while, and then you'll know more about what to do. Freddie didn't kill his daddy. We both know that and, like I said, the Good Lord knows that as well. We'll pray and he'll show us what to do."

Hannah pulled herself up and stood for a moment. The room shifted out of focus and she shook her head. Sarah came to her rescue. "Come on. I'll help you to the kitchen. You can sit down while I make the tea. I think we both need a cup."

Hannah put her hand to her head. "I have a headache, Sarah. Do you think I should take an aspirin?"

Sarah studied her for a minute. "I think you should go to the doctor, Hannah. You hit that floor awfully hard. You could have a concussion."

Hannah argued but when her headache persisted she finally agreed. "Let's take my car, Sarah. It's full of gas."

They ended up at the emergency room of Raleigh General Hospital where Hannah had a CT-scan and Sarah sat beside her until the doctor came back. "You don't have a concussion, but you do have a bruise. I'm going to let you go home and go to bed, but if you still have a headache in the morning, I want you to see a specialist."

"Is it all right for her to take an aspirin?" asked Sarah.

"Yes, and put a cold compress on that side of her head about every ten minutes for a couple of hours." With those instructions, Sarah drove Hannah home where they proceeded to follow the doctor's orders. When Hannah looked comfortable on her sofa Sarah seemed satisfied.

"Hannah, I'm going to my house to check on things, so you lay there and rest until I get back?"

Hannah assured her that she would because her head felt too heavy to do anything else. When Sarah returned she found Hannah sound asleep. She picked up a soft rose-colored afghan on the back of the sofa and spread it gently over Hannah who slept on.

Taking the chair across from Hannah, Sarah sat thinking back over the past few years that had almost killed Hannah. When Hannah and Bill first moved across the street from her on Pike Lane, Sarah felt that she had never seen a more devoted couple. She and Hannah had become fast friends from their very first meeting. Everybody seemed to be drawn to Hannah's rosy outlook on life as well as her feisty determination.

Sarah thought about the first project Hannah took on and smiled. Everybody had said that a group of book lovers like Friends of the Library couldn't be started in their area, but Hannah got that gleam in her eye and with dogged determination got the group organized. The Friends now met faithfully every month. After that, any community problems were often brought to Hannah's door and she jumped right in to help. She wouldn't get involved in politics, though.

"Too many of my friends see things differently than I do and I don't want to lose my friends," was her reply when asked to help on some campaign.

Sarah looked to see if Hannah's breathing was all right as the doctor had advised her, and seeing that she wasn't having any trouble, Sarah went into the kitchen.

"I may as well fix us something to eat. She may be hungry when she wakes up," Sarah mumbled aloud and started opening cupboard doors. As she did this her thoughts were on the trials Hannah was having. The phone rang and she hurried to answer it, not wanting it to wake Hannah.

"Sarah, is Hannah all right? I had a dream about her last night," said the worried voice of Melanie, Hannah's sister-in-law, from the state of Washington. Melanie had talked to Sarah almost as much as she had talked to Hannah during the past two years.

"Melanie, I'm glad you called. Hannah's asleep right now, but this morning she fell and banged her head pretty hard."

"Did she go to the doctor?"

"Yeah, I took her to the emergency room. She didn't have a concussion, but she does have a bad bruise. The doctor said to bring her back tomorrow if she had a headache."

"Why did she fall? Did she trip over something?" Melanie asked.

"No, she was just so shocked and hurt after Freddie was arrested. I think her mind just couldn't handle any more right then."

"Freddie arrested? Why?"

"They accused him of murdering his daddy and took him to jail. He was the last one to see Bill and the first one to find him. That police sergeant said the police chief wanted him arrested because Freddie's finger prints were all over a glass that had poisoned Mylanta in it"

Melanie had listened quietly, but now interrupted. "Oh Lord, for all that to happen in one week! It's no wonder Hannah fainted. Three days ago she found her husband dead and then today they arrest her son. Didn't Freddie tell them he didn't do it?"

"Freddie and Hannah both told the sergeant that they didn't know the Mylanta had anything in it, but they still arrested Freddie. According to what the sergeant said, the chief of police sent him out here to arrest Freddie."

Melanie didn't speak for a moment, and then she said, "Hannah will need somebody with her. I'm surprised she didn't throw something at that sergeant."

Sarah chuckled. "She was too shocked, I guess, so I'm staying with her for a few days, because we both know Hannah. As soon as she gets a little rest she'll be out hunting a lawyer. She won't leave Freddie in jail very long."

CHAPTER 2

WHEN SARAH REVEALED WHAT HAD HAPPENED, Melanie's first thoughts had been of Hannah being alone to deal with all this anguish, but now she knew Sarah would be with her. She sighed with relief.

"Thank you, Sarah. As soon as Cam gets back from his hunting trip we'll try to get a flight out there," said Melanie.

"Hunting trip? Where's he gone to this time? I know he acts as a guide for hunters. Can't you get a message to him?" asked Sarah.

"I'll call the base camp, but they don't take phones when they're on a hunt. It alerts the animals."

From that, Sarah and Melanie began talking about how Hannah was coping. "I hope she'll sell this place," Sarah said. "It was the farm she wanted to come back to when she lived out there, but me and you both know that Bill hated the farm. He was forever trying to get her to sell it, but thank God, Hannah stood her ground on that."

"Yeah, I know. I knew it was the farm all along that she wanted to come back to, but at least she got to visit it even if Bill wouldn't live on it. I'm glad he moved her back there. That was her main conversation while she lived out here," said Melanie.

"Wait just a minute, Melanie. I think I hear Hannah." Sarah walked to the living-room door and stood listening to Hannah's even breathing and then picked up the phone again.

"I think that medicine the doctor gave her had something in it to make her rest. I'm surprised it worked, for most of the time she's like a whirling dervish."

"Well, I hope he did give her something. She won't be still if he didn't" said Melanie. "You've been with her so much more than I have, Sarah, that you know her better than I do anymore."

Sarah smiled. "I guess, you're right, Melanie. For the eighteen years we've known each other, I've almost always been involved in the things they did. They all treated me like their favorite aunt, but I felt like Hannah's mother. I don't know why, I just did."

"I remember Hannah talking about taking you on their camping trips and also you going to "meeting" with her. I never could understand why she didn't say 'church' instead of 'meeting.'"

Sarah laughed. "I thought it was strange at first, but I went with her and Freddie so many times to Zion's Hope Primitive Baptist Church, that I almost felt like a member myself. Bill wouldn't go with her, but me and Freddie did. Of course, if any of my boys came home I didn't go."

"I'd like to know who poisoned that Mylanta. We both know that neither Hannah nor Freddie did it. They both loved Bill too much," said Melanie firmly.

"They certainly did and until Freddie graduated this was the happiest little family I'd ever heard of . . . well, except for the times Bill got into one of those strange moods. I never could figure that out and Hannah didn't know why either. Still, he always came home right after work and he acted like he really loved his family."

Melanie was slow to answer. "Yeah, I thought that too, but according to Hannah, Bill seemed to have changed, but not enough to turn his family against him."

"Well, I guess there are things you don't know about. I always thought that Hannah could buy whatever she wanted, but that sure changed in the last few years. Hannah never was wasteful. I know because I used to go shopping with her."

"He took her checkbook, did you know that?" asked Melanie angrily.

Sarah grimaced. "Yeah, I found out about that and a lot of other things that Hannah had been keeping to herself. I believe it all fell apart when Bill wanted Freddie to date that Henson girl and he did."

Before Melanie hung up she and Sarah had gone over the events of Hannah's life from the first night Freddie stayed out all night. "That was about six months after Sam Henson put Bill over that new project and sent that "hussy" he'd been sleeping with to work with Bill," explained Sarah.

"I guess Bill started sleeping with her too, didn't he?" asked Melanie.

"I don't know if that's when it started, but it did start. The first thing Hannah noticed was Bill drinking. She didn't tell me about it for a long time, but she finally did. I never did say it to her, but I'll bet that's when Bill started fooling around with that woman, too. I don't think conduct like that has ever entered Hannah's mind, though."

Melanie finally hung up. She had assured Sarah that Cam would be calling as soon as he returned from hunting. Sarah finished the meal she had been cooking while talking to Melanie and then went back to check on Hannah. She was still thinking about Bill and that Draper woman and mumbled to herself. "If somebody told her now, she still wouldn't believe that Bill Larkin would look at another woman, but he sure did." Sarah had a scowl on her face as she bent down and patted Hannah on the arm.

"Hannah, Hannah, you need to wake up. I've got supper ready."

Hannah moaned and opened her eyes. "What is it, Sarah? Do you need something?"

Sarah smiled. "I need you to come and help me eat what I've just put on the table."

Hannah looked up and smiled. "I'll eat because I'm going to have to get some strength back or I'll never get you paid for all you're doing." She sat up and swung her feet to the floor.

"Here let me help you. You might get dizzy," said Sarah, grasping her arm as she rose to her feet.

Hannah frowned. "I am weak, but my head feels better and I don't need to be led around like a cripple. I think I must have sloshed some of that muddy water around inside my head." Hannah smiled and squeezed Sarah's hand.

"You had to slosh something around with a lick like that. I guess it's a good thing that carpet is so thick. You head would have bounced if it hadn't been."

Hannah didn't want anything to eat, but she tried because Sarah had prepared such a good meal. She avoided looking across the table to where Freddie always sat. Finally she pushed her chair back and started to rise, to be stopped by Sarah.

"Where are you going? We've not had our dessert yet."

"I'm going to get the phone directory and try to find a lawyer for Freddie. I can't stand the thought of him being in jail."

"The doctor said you should take it easy for awhile. Besides, I've been thinking about a lawyer and I think we need some advice. I don't know which lawyer is good and which one isn't and neither do you. Why don't you just wait 'til tomorrow, maybe the Good Lord will give us some direction about what is best to do."

Hannah felt like the Lord had given her a brain and she needed to do some things for herself. But, not wanting to hurt Sarah, she said, "You're right as usual, Sarah. I'll just wait until tomorrow." Her head was beginning to ache again and she dropped her head in her hands. Sarah grabbed her chin and lifted her head.

Looking her steadily in the eyes, she said, "Hannah, you have to be strong. Crying will only make your head hurt again and you'll still have the same problem."

Hannah reached over and patted Sarah on the arm. "Aw Sarah, you worry too much. I wasn't crying. I've done enough of that this last year to float a battleship. I've got a headache from crying already. You're too good to me and I appreciate it, but don't think I'm going to lie around and moan while you wait on me. That won't solve a thing."

"Well, you don't have to let me wait on you, I'm staying right here and I don't plan to just sit around and do nothing. So whether you're moaning or not I'm going to be here," Sarah replied firmly.

CHAPTER 3

HANNAH SANK BACK INTO HER SEAT and sighed tiredly. Well, I hope no more upsetting things happen, for a few days at least, but I'm glad you've offered to stay a few days. I hate to be such a bother, but I do intend to pay you."

Sarah shook her head and grinned. "You don't have enough money for all I've been doing."

Sarah was as good as her word and Hannah wasn't allowed to do anything at all. When Hannah tried she was taken by the shoulders and marched into the living room. Hannah shook her head at her friend's actions and smiled.

"Thank you, Sarah. I'm glad you're so bossy, but don't let it get to be a habit. You know me and as soon as I gain a little more strength I'll be getting out my rolling pin so I can march down to that courthouse and knock a few heads together."

They both chuckled and Hannah continued with, "I'd feel a lot better right now, if I knew I'd never again hear the name of Civic Enterprise Endeavors."

She wasn't to get her wish, though, for Sabrina Draper rang her doorbell that very same evening. Sarah had gone back to her house for her knitting yarn.

Hannah was shocked when she opened the door and Sabrina introduced herself. She stood stunned for a moment and then with a dangerous gleam in her eyes she spoke up.

"What are you doing here? You sure have a lot of nerve, coming here after you killed my husband. Giving him Mylanta to help his stomach; it helped him to the cemetery. You killed him and now my son is in jail. You're the one who needs to be locked up," stormed Hannah angrily.

Sabrina blanched and stepped back from the door. Shame washed over her as she gazed at this frail, yet beautiful little woman with such sad eyes. Eyes that blazed with anger again when Sabrina said, "I didn't kill your husband, Mrs. Larkin."

"Aren't you the one that gave him the medicine with poison in it?"

"Poison?" Sabrina turned pale. "Mrs. Larkin, I only gave your husband some Mylanta that was given to me. If there was anything in it, I didn't put it there."

"Well, you tell the police who gave it to you. My son is in jail and if you'd give them that information my son would be released."

Sabrina stood in thought for a moment. "It was given to me at a conference. I brought some home for B . . . your husband, since he had been complaining about his stomach."

Hannah looked at her suspiciously, but, at that time, she didn't even think or ask why she was taking medicine to her house for Bill. Hannah was still too weak to stand very long, but her anger held her erect.

"You know who gave it out even if it was at a business conference. If none of the others got sick, then you're the only one that could have put poison in it. I told Sergeant McCauley you should be arrested. My husband is dead and my son has been arrested all because of you."

Hannah was now so white that Sabrina feared she would faint, but instead she looked ready to attack. Hannah managed to stay calm.

"Miss Draper, I hope you're proud of yourself." For the first time in ten years Sabrina Draper was ready to cry, but didn't want this woman to see.

"Well, I can see that you aren't going to believe me. I just wanted you to know that I am really sorry about your husband and I didn't kill him."

"Tell that to the police, Miss Draper. Telling me doesn't help get my son back home," stated Hannah and stepped back from the door.

Sarah had seen the car in Hannah's driveway and hurriedly finished what she was doing in order to get back to Hannah. When she arrived Hannah was still angry and pounding the back of the sofa in frustrated rage.

"Who was in that car that just left here? I saw it and tried to hurry."

Hannah looked up at Sarah. "It was Bill's assistant, that Draper woman. She came to tell me she was sorry about Bill's death. I told her she should be sorry since she killed him. Of course she denied that. She even acted shocked when I mentioned that the Mylanta had poison in it."

"I'll bet she was shocked. These people think they can do anything and never be found out. If she was shocked it was because she'd been caught," said Sarah.

"She's the one that gave it to him, so she'd know if something was in it." Hannah stated.

Sarah nodded her head. "I'll bet she left here scared out of her wits."

"I believe she was. She won't be coming back here. That's for certain," said Hannah and silently hoped that nobody else from CEE showed up.

At nine o'clock the next morning the doorbell rang again. Since Sarah was upstairs Hannah answered it. She opened the door to see a nice-looking, slightly plump lady who looked to be in her fifties. She somehow seemed familiar. "Hello, may I help you?" asked Hannah.

"You don't remember me I know, but I'm Margie Meadows. Your husband introduced us years ago when you were celebrating the news that you were expecting your son," explained the woman.

Hannah gasped in surprise. "Margie Meadows! Yes, I do remember you. My husband always spoke highly of you. Come in. You don't need to stand outside."

Margie entered and looked around at the pleasant room and its furnishings. The walls were a soft off-white and the sofa and one chair were a muted mauve. The other chair was a soft pearly green. These colors were mingled in the drapes, pictures, and the carpet which covered most of the living room floor.

"Sit down here, Miss Meadows," said Hannah pointing to the sofa. "I'll go get us both some coffee. How do you take yours?"

Margie smiled, but noting the pallor and weak condition Hannah was in, said, "Please don't bother, Mrs. Larkin."

"It's no bother, but it may take me a few minutes. I'm a bit slow right now." Hannah stood still, but held onto the sofa.

Margie went to her side. "I'll take coffee if you'll let me go with you to get it. In fact we could drink it in the kitchen."

Hannah smiled and Margie walked by her side to the kitchen. "I'm glad you came. I feel better with someone to talk to . . . I mean I want to talk to someone who liked Bill. I didn't want to talk to that Draper woman, though." Hannah had made it to a chair at the kitchen table and sank thankfully into it.

Margie drew in a surprised breath, but didn't say anything. Instead she smiled. "I'll pour the coffee, if that's all right with you."

Hannah smiled. "Please do. I'm ashamed of my weakness, but my friend, Sarah, says it will get better in a few days."

When they were both seated again, Margie asked, "When did Sabrina Draper come to see you?"

"Yesterday evening. I know it isn't very Christian, but I wanted to hit her. She's the one who gave Bill that Mylanta, but they have arrested my son, Freddie. I think I was pretty rough with her, and I did report her visit to the police." Hannah looked at Margie, whose face had lost all color.

"Are you sick, Miss Meadows?" asked Hannah.

Margie Meadows shook her head, but didn't speak. Hannah rose to her feet, "Let's go in the living room. It's more comfortable in there."

Margie agreed and together they walked back to the living room. Once there with their coffees, Margie, who was seated in a Queen Anne chair at the end of the sofa, turned toward Hannah who had seated herself on the sofa.

"Do you mean they think your son killed his own father?" Margie asked.

"That Sergeant McCauley and another officer came and took him away about four o'clock, day before yesterday. I don't think I could have lived if my neighbor, Sarah Preston, hadn't come to stay with me."

Hannah swallowed her threatening tears and tried to stay calm. "Freddie is as innocent as I am, Miss Meadows, but the sergeant said that since Freddie was the last one to see his dad alive and the first to find him, that the chief wanted him arrested."

Margie Meadows drew in a long breath. "Would you mind telling me all that has happened and especially about Sabrina Draper's visit?"

Hannah looked at this kind woman and asked, "Why do you want to know? We barely know you."

Margie looked very serious. "I'm James Harrison's secretary, and I'm only doing what he can't do himself. A woman can be more help to another woman than a man. Mr. Harrison liked your husband's work and he'll want to know every detail."

Hannah took a drink of coffee and wriggled to a more comfortable position. "Well, as you already know, Sergeant McCauley and his partner arrested Freddie two days after Bill died." Hannah drank more coffee before she continued.

"About six o'clock in the evening on the day they arrested Freddie the doorbell rang. It was Miss Draper, the woman who gave Bill that Mylanta. She's as free as a bird while my Freddie is locked up for what she did. It isn't fair, Miss Meadows, and if I have to, I'll sell everything here to get Freddie out of jail," said Hannah grimly.

Margie left her seat and came over to sit beside of Hannah as if drawn to her. She sat quietly for a moment and then said, "Could . . . Would you tell me about your life with Bill. Sometimes it helps to talk about the good things when some tragedy happens."

Hannah's mother would have said the same thing, and Hannah found herself telling Margie about her begging Bill to move back to West Virginia with her, about buying their house, and the joy they'd shared with Freddie."

Suddenly she stopped and looked at Margie in a puzzled manner. "I didn't mean to tell you the story of my whole life. I'm sorry."

"No, no. I suppose I've gotten way out of line by asking you to talk about Bill so soon. Please forgive me," said Margie uneasily.

Hannah sat thinking that she certainly felt better, having talked about all the good years. She smiled. "Thanks. I do feel better and I felt you really cared."

Margie looked relieved. "I do care, Mrs. Larkin. Bill Larkin has always had . . . such a good name in the company. We also know that Sabrina Draper is . . . was his assistant."

Hannah looked hurt and angry. "I'd never met her before, but I'd sure heard Bill talk about her enough and I didn't like her. While she was here, I just felt like she was trying to cover up something. Does that make sense?"

Margie sat thinking. "Well, I wasn't here, so I don't know about that, but some people pick up on things others can't. What did the police say when you told them about Ms. Draper's visit?"

"They just said that they appreciated me calling and that they were checking every angle." Hannah and Margie sat as if in thought until Hannah continued.

"Miss Meadows, Freddie is not important in this town. That woman may be. Or she may have some ties to somebody important. I'm afraid they'll pin this on Freddie," complained Hannah.

"Try not to worry, dear. I'm not important either, but I know some people who carry a lot of weight around here. I'll see what I can find out. In the meantime, I'm going to find your son a good lawyer," said Margie as she rose from the sofa.

Hannah looked at Margie curiously. "Why would you do that, Miss Meadows? This has nothing to do with you. Freddie and I shouldn't matter to you. I know you and Bill worked for the same company, but that's no reason for you to help us. I'm fairly sure Bill had insurance that will pay for a lawyer. I just don't know how to get a good one."

Margie hesitated before saying, "You're right. I hardly know you, but working with Bill for over twenty years makes me care. Bill was a fine man and I would like to be of some help. My boss will know all the good lawyers. I'll ask him to give me contact information if you like."

Hannah smiled wearily. "Yes, please do. Sarah and I asked the Lord to send us some help and He has. You're welcome any time you want to stop by."

Margie smiled and thanked her before picking up her handbag from the floor and letting herself out the door.

CHAPTER 4

WHEN SARAH CAME DOWN THE STAIRS she saw Margie's back going out the door. "Who was that?"

"That was Margie Meadows. She is secretary to James Harrison, the president of CEE. Bill introduced us when I first learned I was pregnant with Freddie. She said she'd ask her boss for help in getting a good lawyer for Freddie."

"Well great! Somebody in her position would know more about who is a good lawyer and who isn't than you or I would." Sarah said as she headed for the kitchen to cook breakfast.

That evening Hannah's doorbell rang again and she warily answered it. She, at first, started to slam the door in the face of the man standing there, but thought he might have news of Freddie. Sergeant Keith McCauley was standing with his hat in his hand.

"Hello, Mrs. Larkin. I stopped by to see if you are all right. I know how upset you are about your husband and your son. I am so sorry all of this has happened to you. I know it's hard to lose your companion." The sergeant seemed to be nervous, which surprised her. He stood looking down at her as if he was seeing an angel.

Hannah had no idea of the image she made and wouldn't have cared if she had. She was so tired and worried about Freddie that she hadn't even bothered with her hair all day. Now she pushed it back from her face and looked up at Keith.

"My husband was . . . a major part of my life for over twenty years. He's gone, but my son needs my help. I'd be all right if I could have Freddie back home where he belongs. My son did not m . . . hurt his father."

Keith McCauley wanted to fold her in his arms and protect her from all this pain, but instead said, "I just stopped by to let you know that I'll do everything I possibly can to make it easy on your son. I saw him today and thought you'd want to know how he's doing. He's in a cell by himself and is confident that he will be out soon."

"Did you actually see Freddie and talk to him?" Hannah had a puzzled look on her face.

"Yes, I took him some reading material and some snacks this morning, and Freddie asked me to come out and check on you. He said to tell you not to worry and that he is fine and is being treated well."

Hannah only came up to Keith's shoulder. *She looks like a small, bewildered fairy*, thought Keith as she stood staring up at him.

"I'm glad they're treating him good since that Draper woman is the guilty one. Freddie shouldn't have been arrested. How much do I owe you for the snacks?" Hannah had a stubborn set to her jaw.

Keith's eyes widened in surprise, "Owe me! You don't owe me anything. I just wanted to take him something. He's a good boy and I hope he gets out soon to be here with you, Mrs. Larkin. You have a fine son."

Hannah looked startled. "Sergeant, I'm not stupid. Policemen don't care enough to visit inmates or their families, so what do you really want? I guess you think I'll tell you something you missed when you arrested Freddie." Hannah knew she sounded sarcastic but didn't care since she was still hurt and suspicious.

Keith listened to what she said and realized that this small, delicate, and beautiful woman didn't trust him and didn't like him either.

She's going to hate me unless I can change the way she feels, he thought as he looked down into her still angry upturned face.

"Mrs. Larkin, honestly, I stopped by today because Freddie asked me to and I wanted to anyway. I truly believe your son is innocent. I saw the anguish you went through at your husband's death and I understood. I lost my wife ten years ago, and it reminded me of how much pain one has when a companion dies. I'd like to help make this all a little easier if I could," said Keith.

Hannah's cheeks turned a delicate pink and her look softened a bit. "Thank you for that at least. I'm going to see Freddie tomorrow. He and I need to make funeral arrangements for my husband."

Before he could stop himself, Keith blurted, "You don't need to be driving, Mrs. Larkin. I'll come by after my shift is over and drive you to see Freddie."

Hannah's eyes glared angrily. "No thanks. I don't want to ride in a patrol car. The neighbors will think I've been arrested also."

"I wouldn't come in a patrol car. I can bring my own car, if you'll allow me to drive you to town," said Keith. Hannah noticed that he had kind-looking brown eyes.

"I don't need you to come, Sergeant. My friend, Sarah Preston, will drive me. Thanks for stopping by," Hannah said in a dismissive tone.

Keith clamped his lips together, put his hat back on his head and turned. "I'll tell Freddie you seem all right and that you plan to visit tomorrow. If I can be of any assistance let me know."

The sergeant turned from the door and was soon down the steps and in his car. Hannah stood with the door open for a moment and then slammed it shut with as much force as she could muster.

"The nerve of that man, coming here as if he thought I'd be glad to see him," muttered Hannah as Sarah came into the living room.

"Did I hear someone talking?"

"You sure did. You heard that police sergeant that arrested Freddie," said Hannah.

"What'd he want? He shouldn't come here. Now you're all upset again," said Sarah.

"Oh, he said he wanted to let me know that Freddie was fine, but I don't trust him and I let him know it too."

"Well, don't let him upset you. We know that the Good Lord sent Miss Meadows and when she gets that lawyer you won't have to be so afraid. Freddie will be home in a few more days. I just know he will."

"He didn't upset me, but I'm as mad as a hornet right now. He should be out arresting that Draper woman instead of nosing around out here. He thinks I know something else I guess or may think I killed Bill. Leaning back tiredly on the sofa, Hannah closed her eyes and saw Freddie's face when he was arrested.

She quickly opened her eyes again as fear like a great gulf surrounded her. Hannah shuddered and turned her thoughts to the Lord. *Lord, help me to be strong so I can help my son,* she prayed and suddenly that thought took such a grasp on her mind that she seemed to gain strength. She sat up straighter and made up her mind to try harder.

Sarah had been urging her to eat more and she knew she needed to eat in order to regain her strength. So, when they were eating supper that night she tried to eat as much food as she could.

"Eat this piece of chicken. It'll give you the protein you need," Sarah coaxed as she pushed the plate in front of Hannah.

The plate contained a mixture of broccoli and carrots, creamed potatoes, a piece of chicken, and a dinner roll. Hannah looked at it and was surprised that it looked tempting.

"It's a shame to eat a nice looking meal like this. You certainly make food look appetizing. This would make a nice commercial for a healthy meal."

Sarah smiled and sat down across from Hannah. "If food doesn't look nice I'm not interested in eating it, even in nice restaurants."

Hannah sat eating and thinking about how long it had been since she had eaten in a restaurant. "It's been so long since I've eaten in a restaurant that I wouldn't know how to conduct myself."

"I know it must have been a year or more since you and Bill had gone out anywhere, or so it seemed to me."

Hannah paused with her fork lifted. "It had been two years or more since Bill and I had gone anywhere together, and not often before that. It seems that from the time Freddie met Nicole Henson, Bill became a boarder in our home."

"That's when he started staying away at night, wasn't it?" Sarah got up to get the two desserts from the refrigerator.

"I know this all started the night after Freddie had stayed out all night for the first time ever. Bill seemed to change so much from that time on. It got so bad that I dreaded for him to come home. It was soon after that when he took the check book," Hannah recalled.

"Bill never knew that I moved half of our savings into a private account with only my name on it. That was the money from the sale of Dad and Mom's house in the state of Washington, Sarah. It was really my money anyway and he couldn't have done anything if he had found out, but he would have cursed and threatened."

Sarah sat with one bite of pie left to eat. "He was drinking quite a bit, too, wasn't he?"

Hannah pushed back her plate. "Yes, and Sarah, I don't want you to ever tell this, but I found a bag of something that I felt was cocaine in his sock drawer. I thought Freddie might have put it there to aggravate Bill. When I thought about it, though, I realized that Freddie couldn't have put it there, at that time, for he had already left home. So, maybe Bill was using drugs too. God, I don't know. I do know that for the last two years he became somebody I didn't even know."

"Did you still love him, Hannah?"

Hannah sat deep in thought. "No, I didn't love that stranger that was here the past two years. He was so hateful, neglectful, and even at times dangerous. The Bill I knew and fell in love with back in Washington has been gone for a long time, Sarah. Sergeant McCauley said he understood my pain since he had lost his wife ten years ago. I hope their love hadn't died like mine did. Of course I brought all of my pain on myself because of my love of West Virginia."

"No, you didn't, Hannah. Love doesn't cause awful things to happen. I know you said you felt guilty, but I can't really see how any of this has been your fault. You didn't tell Bill to take on that project that Sam Henson put him over and you didn't start him to drinking either."

Hannah sat in a reflective mood. "No I didn't, Sarah. In fact I begged him to not take on some of the things Sam Henson pushed his way."

"Aye, well. What's done is done and you'll have Freddie back in a few days. Now he's back to being the same sweet, kind, loving young man he has always been," said Sarah, nodding with satisfaction, as she took both of their plates to the sink.

"Sarah, Miss Meadows said she would ask her boss about a good lawyer and would hire him if I wanted her to, but I don't think she's had time to do anything yet, do you? Of course, I think it's so strange that she'd even want to. She doesn't really know us."

"Hannah, don't look a gift horse in the mouth. You asked for help and she said she'd help and it doesn't matter what her motives are." Sarah turned to the sink with her stack of plates and bowls.

"Let's leave the dishes until after the six o'clock news. They may have arrested Miss Draper," said Hannah in a hopeful voice.

"I'll make us a cup of hot chocolate if you'll drink one with me," said Sarah. Hannah agreed and soon they were in the living-room on each end of the sofa since the end tables were so useful to hold their chocolate while it cooled a bit.

Channel 8 news was on and the death of Bill Larkin was the major headline. Sergeant Keith McCauley was being interviewed. He talked about the case and answered questions. Both Hannah and Sarah paid rapt attention and Hannah caught her breath at the first question. "Is Freddie Larkin the only suspect?" asked a man with NBC News.

"No, he isn't. This case is like a spider web and the police department feels that the untangling will reach much farther than Freddie Larkin."

"Well, it looks like they have a number of suspects, doesn't it? What do you reckon he meant by it being like a spider web?" Sarah looked at Hannah narrowly.

"I'm not sure, Sarah, but I'll bet that Draper woman is the 'black widow spider.' She could trap just about any man. She is pretty, but I didn't believe a word she said," Hannah said grimly.

CHAPTER 5

WHEN SABRINA DRAPER WALKED DOWN HANNAH Larkin's drive that evening, Hannah had no way of knowing that her angry accusation flung at the woman would set off a mad flurry of activity. If she had followed Sabrina Draper though, she would have been astonished at the 'spider's web' of dishonesty and deceit in which that young woman was entangled. Piece by piece the unraveling was slowly being revealed and almost every person that had any contact with CEE was living with dread in some way.

Of course Hannah didn't know, and couldn't follow Sabrina, but as is usually the case when evil schemes are underway, nothing goes unnoticed. Even though Hannah never once thought of following Sabrina Draper, another person certainly did.

Sabrina Draper walked away from Hannah's door more upset than she had ever been in her life. Trying to determine the best strategy, she drove aimlessly around town. Finally she made a decision and when she found a pay phone booth, she stopped. She got out of the car and looked up and down the street before entering the booth. She dialed a number.

"Hello," said a modulated voice that sounded perturbed.

"I know you told me not to call except in emergencies, but I just wanted you to know that I went to see Mrs. Larkin this morning and . . ."

Sabrina was interrupted by a startled gasp. "You did what?"

"I went to see Mrs. Larkin this morning. I was sorry that Bill died. Besides, I was the one who gave him that Mylanta. It had poison in it. Did you know that? I know I did not put poison in it, but I think I know who did." Sabrina said as she stood waiting.

"Did you mention my name, Miss Draper?" asked a more normal voice.

"No, I didn't, but Mrs. Larkin has told the police that I did it. I'm not taking the blame for murder-not for any price," Sabrina said sternly.

"Of course, you're not. Nobody would ask you to do something like that. For the record, I did not and do not know who doctored the Mylanta."

"Well, Margie Meadows brought the bottles into the meeting and told people to take two each. I don't think she knows anything about poisons," replied Sabrina.

There was a pause on the other end. "Where are you calling from, Miss Draper?"

"I'm in a phone booth. I'm afraid my phone may be tapped, since I'm sure Mrs. Larkin wasted no time in notifying the police," answered Sabrina.

"Miss Draper, go home and act as if nothing has happened. If the police come, just tell them the truth without naming any names. I'll get busy on this end to see what needs to be done. Can you do that?"

Sabrina almost slumped with relief. "Sure, Mr . . . . I'll do what you say but get this all settled, please."

Again, Sabrina looked up and down the street and then hurried back into her car. She started the engine and pulled back into the traffic, letting out some of her anxiety in a long breath. She didn't see the battered, green, Buick station wagon that slid into traffic three cars behind her.

When she reached her apartment, she got out in the downstairs garage, closed and locked the doors, and went to the lift which would take her to her second floor apartment. She hadn't seen another car pull into the garage, but as she entered the lift, a man suddenly appeared and stepped into the lift with her.

Sabrina looked at him suspiciously. Quaking inside, she quickly pressed the up button on the control panel. Sabrina drew in her breath and stood gripping her purse by one end, prepared for use as a weapon. Never having seen the man before, she didn't know how to act. Finally she said, "Hello."

The man looked at her, but gave no reply. Sabrina could taste fear in her mouth.

The lift stopped, the door opened, and Sabrina got out. "Who are you?" Sabrina asked fearfully as she put distance between herself and the stranger.

The lift door closed and left Sabrina still standing there. She looked at the buttons and saw that the down button was lit. *He just rode up with me and then went back down again. That does not make any sense at all*, she thought, petrified with fear.

Sabrina sped into her apartment and quickly locked the door. She kicked off her shoes and padded across to the window. Looking down, she saw the man getting into an old green station wagon. Dread hung over her like a pall. "He can't live in this building and drive a car like that," she said aloud and shivered in fright.

So many things were happening, and Sabrina felt trapped in the middle of it all. She wondered about the phone call she had made to Mr . . . She had droned it into her head never to say his name, and now she wouldn't even think it. He was always Mr. Blank and on the phone he had said he didn't know about the Mylanta. Somebody did, that was certain. Margie Meadows had boxes of it at the meeting, so somebody had to provide it. *I guess I could ask Miss Meadows, but I've not spoken to her over twice since I've been working for CEE,* she thought.

Sabrina made a salad for her dinner and was just about ready to sit down and eat when her phone rang. When she picked up the receiver she couldn't even say hello before Sam Henson's voice rapped out. "So, you reported me to the police, did you? Well, if I go down you'll go along with me, and I'm not talking about Bill's death. You had to go running out to tell Mrs. Larkin a sob story and opened up a bigger keg of worms than you bargained for, you sneaking bitch," Sam snarled.

"What are you talking about, Sam? I didn't report anybody or mention anybody's name when I went to see Mrs. Larkin! You must be losing your mind," Sabrina shouted.

"Then you don't deny that you went to see Mrs. Larkin?" snarled Sam.

"No, but how did you know? Are you spying on me again?" questioned Sabrina angrily.

"Sure, I am having you watched, you double-crossing whore! I was the greatest man alive as long as I was helping you move up the ladder, but now you've found bigger fish to fry. Well, I'll tell you this, if my name becomes involved in this investigation of Bill Larkin's death, I'm coming after you. You can count on it. I would be really careful if I were you," threatened Sam slamming down the receiver.

Sabrina sat in stunned silence. *He thinks I know more than I do. I know he was padding the accounts, and I know he has contacts with drug dealers, but I can't prove any of it. By his talk, he thinks I know a lot more than I do, and he's acting scared.* She shivered in fear. She knew that people could do strange things when they were scared.

Sabrina couldn't eat her salad. After a few bites she ran to the bathroom and lost it all as she hung over the commode. Finally she straightened up and her first thought was, "I need a lawyer."

When she felt a little better, she picked up the phone book. She finally settled on Stuart & Stuart, on North Eisenhower Drive. She dialed their number and, although it was now six o'clock, she got an appointment for the next morning at ten.

When her nausea eased, she fixed a scrambled egg sandwich and sat down in front of the television to eat it.

The six o'clock news was now on and the Bill Larkin murder case was the main focus. Sergeant Keith McCauley was being interviewed. "This case is tangled like a spider's web with many, many links. Right now Mr. Larkin's son is being held for questioning, but he isn't the only suspect."

Sergeant McCauley then took other questions, but Sabrina had already heard enough to make her too sick to eat.

"They'll be here to arrest me. I know they will. I didn't put anything in that Mylanta, but if they didn't believe his son, they certainly won't believe me," she mumbled in a quivery voice.

Just before his shift was over that evening Sergeant Keith McCauley met a new addition to the Beckley Police Force, Special Investigator Steve Hammer. Sergeant McCauley didn't know who had called in the special investigator. He knew the chief hadn't, since he had cursed a blue streak when Steve Hammer showed up. Keith was glad, though, because Steve had worked all over the country on different cases and would certainly be a lot of help. Now there would be two people assiduously searching every clue presented and they should be able to make some headway. *Maybe if I can help get Freddie Larkin out of jail his mother will stop hating me,* thought Sergeant McCauley.

Back at the Larkin residence, Sarah and Hannah talked as they prepared for bed. They planned to visit Freddie the next day.

"Wouldn't it be wonderful, Sarah, if a lawyer could get Freddie released and we could bring him home tomorrow?"

"I told you the Lord is in control and he knows Freddie is innocent, so yes, it would be wonderful if he's released, but I wouldn't build up any hopes. I don't want you to be disappointed," cautioned Sarah.

"I hate to go inside a jail, but I can't wait to see Freddie," said Hannah. "Have you ever been in a jail, Sarah?"

"No, I was going to visit my cousin there once but he was released before I went." Sarah looked across at Hannah.

"Now don't get your hopes up. He probably won't get out tomorrow. Let's just concentrate on getting these funeral arrangements made."

Hannah sighed. "It's hard to be patient when your child is in trouble, but I'll try." She looked at Sarah and tried to smile. "Now let's get back to the funeral. I'd like to hold Bill's funeral at Zion's Hope Primitive Baptist Church, but it is really too small if any of Bill's co-workers want to attend. What do you think, Sarah?"

"Well, since Bill wouldn't go there to church, I guess I'd just take him to a funeral home and have the funeral there. Their chapels are always large." Sarah hesitated. "Why don't you just ask Freddie and do whatever he suggests."

Hannah and Sarah continued to talk about the many things they had done together. "Bill liked having you with us, Sarah. I've often thought he treated you like a close relative."

Sarah smiled. "Yeah he did. I think Bill really liked me, but . . . I . . . I don't think Bill really liked many people. Am I wrong?"

Hannah was quiet for a few minutes. "I thought he really liked Cam, but he tried to fight Cam when his parents were killed."

Seeing that this kind of talk was making Hannah sad, Sarah said, "We don't need to worry about that now. We just need to take care of you and Freddie."

They were unaware of it, but several people who had worked with Bill were getting very uneasy, especially after listening to the six o'clock news on Channel 8 that evening.

Hannah switched off the television and said, "Sarah, somebody in CEE killed Bill and now the most innocent person that could be found has been arrested. I guess it's like everything else, it's who you know and how much clout you have, isn't it?"

"Now don't get discouraged, Hannah. That Meadows woman works for James Harrison and you know how often his name is in the papers. He's a real important person."

"Sarah, if Miss Meadows gets a good lawyer, Freddie should be out on bail fairly soon, don't you think? His being locked up is breaking my heart, but I'll not let him know it. I know that some of those people Bill worked with are powerful in the county and maybe the state as well. They could probably pay a judge to pin this on Freddie unless he has a really good lawyer. I wish I didn't know about how dishonest the world has gotten. It makes me not trust anybody."

Sarah looked at Hannah and shook her head. "God's more powerful than anybody in CEE. He'll see us through. We just need to have faith and wait."

CHAPTER 6

IN ANOTHER PART OF TOWN SAM Henson was not showing his usual smiling, jovial, "big shot" self. He was one of the watchers of the Channel 8 interview, and when he heard that poison had been found in Mylanta it made him very uneasy. He sat still as a mouse, but he was thinking furiously. *I've never used what Martha and I learned many years ago, but now may be the time.*

Sam got up and went into the dining room, through the kitchen, and onto the patio, his ears tuned to any sound. Not hearing a sound in the house, he slipped quietly back to his study and closed the door. He picked up the phone and dialed. When a voice on the other end answered, Sam put a handkerchief over the mouthpiece and in a high-pitched voice said, "Once the CEE Corporation had a retreat in the Adirondack Mountains, and a certain man was seen in the arms of another gentleman. I wouldn't want to reveal the other gentleman's name." Sam quietly hung up, and taking his handkerchief, he wiped the perspiration from his forehead and went back to the living room.

When his wife, Martha, came in, he looked up and smiled. "When I retire, how would you like to spend two weeks in Hawaii?"

Martha was stunned. "You've either lost your mind or finally opened your eyes to the fact that you have a family. Which is it?"

Sam smiled. "Well, I was just thinking about poor old Bill Larkin. He worked like a dog, and what did it get him? I guess I just thought I'd better start doing some things with you and Nicole while I still have the chance."

Martha came and sat beside him on the sofa. "Did you see the news interview with Sergeant McCauley? I feel so sorry for Bill's wife and son. Sam, I don't think his son put poison in that Mylanta. Where would a kid like that get poison? I wouldn't know where to get something like that. Would you?"

Sam looked startled for a moment. "No, no I wouldn't have any idea. It's probably not the son, but who could have done that? I hear that the police are questioning Sabrina Draper, but she wouldn't know where to get poison either, I don't think," Sam replied.

"Well, she knows how to use men to get what she wants. I wouldn't put her past anything. She's nothing but a classy whore in my book. I hope it's her, or she'll try to break up some other home," said Martha bitterly.

Not wanting to get into a fight about Sabrina Draper again, Sam quickly said, "I guess we should send condolences to Mrs. Larkin. We'll attend the funeral, of course. All the CEE people will attend, I think. At least I think they should, since he has worked for our corporation for twenty years."

They were both startled when the doorbell rang. "Were you expecting anyone?" Sam asked Martha as he arose to answer the door.

"It's probably somebody for you. None of my friends would dare call at this time of day," replied Martha. They all knew she usually napped for two hours most afternoons.

When Sam opened the door, there stood Sergeant McCauley. "Well, hello, Sergeant. What can I do for you?" Sam asked, trying to sound jovial.

Behind the sergeant was another man Sam didn't recognize, but he assumed he was a new man on the Beckley police force.

"Sam, we'd like to talk to you," stated Sergeant McCauley.

"Come in! Can't leave Beckley's finest standing outside," said Sam with a laugh as he stepped back to let them in.

Both men walked inside to be met by Martha. "Martha, this is Sergeant McCauley of the Beckley police and I don't know this gentleman," Sam said, looking at Sergeant McCauley expectantly.

"This is Special Investigator Steve Hammer, a federal investigator," explained Sergeant McCauley.

Sam's eyes widened and Martha gasped in surprise. Martha tried to cover her gasp with a smile. "Hello Sergeant and Mr. Hammer." She gave an almost imperceptible nod at the other man while keeping her eyes on Sergeant McCauley.

Sam Henson thought, *somebody is on to something, but who called in the Feds?*

"Would you like to go into the living room where we can be more comfortable?" asked Martha, nodding her head in the direction of the room leading from the foyer.

McCauley and Hammer followed the Hensons into the living room and took a seat on the sofa. Sam and Martha sat on a loveseat across from them.

Sergeant McCauley looked at Sam. "I'm sure you know why we are here, don't you, Sam?"

"I guess it's to question me about the Larkin case? Ask away. I'll answer as best I can," replied Sam. Turning to look at Martha, who had turned very pale, he asked, "Does Martha have to be in on this? She knows nothing at all about CEE."

Both men looked at Martha, and seeing her pallor looked at each other. Sergeant McCauley said, "Mrs. Henson, it's your choice. Whatever you want to do is all right with us."

Martha looked at Sam and wondered if there was something he didn't want her to know. She sat up straighter and looked directly at Sergeant McCauley. "I'm all right. I would like to stay."

Both men looked at Sam. "I just didn't want her to get upset," he said as he shrugged his shoulders.

Sergeant McCauley pulled out a pen and a small notepad. "Sam, for the record, you are the Project Coordinator for all the businesses sponsored by CEE, is that right?"

"That's right. I, with all the other administrative departments, get all the businesses off and running before we turn them loose to fend for themselves," replied Sam.

"Then you are over the Blennoc Project?" asked Steve Hammer.

"I was until two years ago," stated Sam.

"Who took it over then?" Hammer asked.

"I turned it over to Bill Larkin."

"Why?" asked Hammer.

Sam shifted in his chair, cleared his throat, looked at Martha then drew in a deep breath. "Martha didn't like my assistant."

"Do you mean Sabrina Draper?"

Sam shuffled his feet and mumbled in the affirmative.

Martha gasped. "Sam Henson you know . . . "started Martha and then seemed to not know what to say. She continued with, "I only wanted you home more."

Sergeant McCauley looked searchingly at Martha. "Were you jealous of his assistant, Mrs. Henson?"

"Have you met Sabrina Draper, Sergeant? She's enough to turn any man's head, especially an old coot who wants to stay young," snorted Martha indignantly.

Steve Hammer interrupted. "Mr. Henson, what do you know about cyanide poison?"

Both Martha's and Sam's eyes were blaring. "What do you mean? I know that there is a cyanide poison and that's about all," blurted Sam. "Are you accusing me of something?"

"We're not accusing anyone right now, Sam. We're just investigating every angle," explained Sergeant McCauley.

"Mr. Henson, you did furnish the Mylanta that was handed out at a conference about two months ago, didn't you?" asked Hammer with a narrow piercing look.

Sam blanched. "Who told you that?"

Steve Hammer calmly said, "We are talking to a lot of people."

"I sent a case or two of Mylanta to that meeting as samples. We do that all the time. The conference was on dealing with stress in the workplace. A lot of people took home samples. We've not had any complaints. In fact, several people called to thank us for providing the Mylanta.

"You arrested Bill Larkin's son, didn't you? If you arrested him why are you still out looking for someone else?" asked Martha.

"He says he didn't do it. His lawyer will have him out as soon as he gets a bail hearing," replied Steve Hammer.

Both Hammer and McCauley asked several more questions, before rising to leave. "Don't worry, folks we will unravel this whole mess. Who knows what may turn up?" This was Hammer's parting shot as they walked out the door.

Martha closed the door quietly and turned to Sam. "With those two working on the case I don't think Bill Larkin's son will be in jail very long, do you?"

CHAPTER 7

Civic Enterprise Endeavors was operating as if the murder of one of their employees was a daily occurrence. Margie Meadows was there every day, even though Bill Larkin's death had shaken her to the core. The day after Margie had heard the news she had gone to visit Hannah Larkin. On that visit she'd promised Hannah she'd get a good lawyer for Freddie and that promise stayed on her mind.

She went home thinking she would ask Mr. Harrison for help, but he was in a meeting all the next day. On the following day he had to leave for a three-day conference on small business development. Margie knew she had a lot of things to do, but she felt it was urgent to ask James Harrison about a good lawyer for Freddie Larkin.

Mr. Harrison came by the office before leaving for the airport and Margie hurried into his office.

"Mr. Harrison, I have a big favor to ask of you. If you have five minutes, I'd appreciate it."

Mr. Harrison looked at her in a speculative manner and stood quietly waiting.

"Can you help me get a good lawyer for Bill Larkin's son? His son didn't kill him and Bill's wife has been ill herself." Margie stood with her hands clasped together in front of her chest and Mr. Harrison could tell she was nervous.

"You're really interested in this case, aren't you, Margie? Is there a particular reason?"

Margie turned pale. "There is, Mr. Harrison, but if you don't mind I'd rather not talk about it. When this is all over I may tell you. I've never told anyone else, but I think I could tell you."

Mr. Harrison rose from his seat. "I'll listen, Margie, but I can wait." He stood looking at her solemnly.

"I'm going to do something I've never done before. I'm going to call my own lawyer and get him on the case to defend the Larkin boy. How does that sound? I'll call him, but you'll have to fill him in or wait until I get back."

Margie jumped to her feet and reached out her hands to him as tears streamed from her eyes. Mr. Harrison took both of her hands in his. "You really care about people, don't you, Margie Meadows?"

Margie was too emotional to answer, but she looked at Mr. Harrison from adoring eyes.

"Margie, if I'd ever decided to marry I would have looked for someone just like you. You are a special woman." Mr. Harrison released her hands and returned to his seat behind the desk.

"This man's name is Jerome Judson and there's not a better lawyer in the state of West Virginia. He'll have that boy home in no time." Margie stood still staring at him in wonder and relief.

James Harrison picked up the phone, but held it in his hand until Margie realized he was waiting for her to leave.

"Thanks, Mr. Harrison. I'll never forget this. Freddie is as innocent as a lamb." She walked out of his office and made straight for the bathroom where she sat for several minutes sobbing softly. Then she washed her face and put on more makeup.

When Mr. Harrison came to give her the news that Judson was on the case Margie was industriously taking care of the office business. One part of her mind, though, was on Hannah and Freddie Larkin.

"I hope this lawyer can get Freddie out soon," she mumbled just as Mr. Harrison came out of his office and into hers.

"Margie, Judson will talk to the Larkin boy within the next day or two and since Bill Larkin was an employee here, you can tell Mrs. Larkin that his fees will be paid by the company."

"But, Mr. Harrison, we've never done this before. Won't the stockholders raise a ruckus?"

Mr. Harrison smiled. "Margie I didn't say to tell the newspaper that the company will pay the fees, but you can tell Mrs. Larkin that. Let's say this is my gift to you."

Margie's eyes filled with tears again and Mr. Harrison shook his head. "No more tears, Margie. I have too many things on my mind. Let's just bide our time. Judson won't let us down."

"Have a good trip, Mr. Harrison," said Margie to his departing back as he strode out of her office without comment.

Well, I guess Freddie will have to stay at least three more days, thought Margie as she picked up the telephone directory. She still had James Harrison on her mind. She sat for a moment doodling on her pad, and ended up with a picture of James's face. She ran her finger down the funeral parlor page and drew a line beneath one name. She picked up the phone and punched in Hannah Larkin's number.

Sarah answered. "Hello, Sarah Preston speaking."

"Sarah! Oh, you are Mrs. Larkin's friend, aren't you? Miss Preston, this is Margie Meadows. Has Mrs. Larkin told you about me?"

"Miss Meadows, I was planning to call you. I wanted to thank you for all the help you're being to Hannah. She's been through so much and your willingness to find her a lawyer for her son has taken a big load off her shoulders. You did get a lawyer, didn't you?"

"Yes, Freddie has a lawyer, but I didn't do much to get him. I just happened to be working for a man with a lot of good connections, like James Harrison. He's the one who made the call and now Freddie will have the best lawyer in West Virginia representing him," said Margie, sounding pleased.

"Well, at least you got one. Hannah didn't know who to trust and she knew she could trust you. If you say he's a good lawyer that's good enough for us," said Sarah.

"He is very good, Mrs. Preston, and I'm very pleased that he took the case, even though he probably won't get to do much for two or three days Mr. Harrison will be away and I don't know Mr. Judson."

Sarah breathed a sigh of relief. "Thank you so much. Hannah and I are going to see Freddie today. She wants to talk to him about finalizing funeral arrangements for his dad."

"That will be so hard on both of them. I'm glad you'll be with them, Mrs. Preston.

"Just call me Sarah. Anybody that's good to Hannah is a friend to me as well. I love that young woman."

"Well, then we'll just be Sarah and Margie. How's that?"

"That suits me just fine Miss uh . . . Margie. I like that fine."

"What if I call you tonight just to see how the arrangements go? I might be able to help some. I don't see how Hannah is holding up like she is. You can tell by watching her that she going on nerve alone. She must have a lot of faith."

"She has that all right." Sarah turned to watch Hannah descending the stairs and smiled before turning back to the phone.

"That will be fine, Margie. You should see Hannah right now. She's awfully pretty even if she does sometimes need a cane to walk with, but she'd die before she'd admit it. Well, okay then. I'll be expecting your call around seven. Bye."

Sarah, with Hannah settled snugly in the passenger seat, drove slowly down town. Once inside city hall, Hannah asked to see Freddie Larkin and they were told to take a seat.

"Someone is with him right now. You can see your son when the visitor leaves," said the officer in charge.

Hannah and Sarah sat side by side, not speaking since they neither knew what to expect. "Do you think that's the lawyer with him, Sarah?" Hannah whispered, leaning close to Sarah.

Sarah shrugged her shoulders. "I'm afraid to hope, but it might be."

Both women sat looking around at the austerity as to furniture and pictures, and every person they saw looked glum. Sarah leaned close to Hannah again and whispered. "They all look like they'd rather not be here. That Chief Donaldson must be a devil to work for."

Before Hannah could reply, a door opened and a tall man with a briefcase came through. He nodded at them and strode quickly from the building.

The same officer who had first spoken to them came through a door in the hallway and motioned to them. Hannah and Sarah quickly walked to his side.

"I'll take you ladies to see Mr. Larkin, but you can't take your purses in with you unless we see all the contents." Both women sighed in exasperation and handed their purses to the officer. He emptied each purse onto a table one at a time. Soon everything was back in each purse and they were told to follow the officer.

They were led down the hall and into a room with a partition made of opaque glass down the middle. Every three feet there was an opening in the partition like a letter slot, but wider. Each opening had a little bench in front of it. Hannah and Sarah were led to a bench and told to wait and the officer left. The two women sat looking through the opening in front of them and were relieved when Freddie came walking toward them.

Freddie walked slowly over to the bench and sat down. When he saw his mother and Sarah he gulped. "Mom, I didn't expect you this early. Aunt Sarah thanks for bringing Mom. His face was wreathed in a big smile. He put his hand through the slot and Hannah put her hand through from the other side. Their hands clasped in such a loving hold that Sarah blinked back her threatening tears. She saw that even in her pale trembling state Hannah wasn't crying and was proud.

"Freddie, your mother is still weak and probably shouldn't have come, but she wanted to talk to you about the funeral arrangements for your daddy." Sarah turned to Hannah.

Hannah straightened to a very erect position and smiled. "I'm all right. Seeing Freddie incarcerated hurts, but he'll be out before long."

"That's the spirit, Mom. Aunt Sarah is right. I have a lawyer now, a Jerome Judson. He sent his assistant to get some information just a few minutes ago. You may have seen him." Freddie released his tight clasp but still held Hannah's hand.

Hannah choked back any tears that fought to get through. "I suppose we did. A tall man with a briefcase came to the front and nodded to us as he went out."

Sarah spoke up. "Freddie, your mom has made the funeral arrangements, but she feels she needs your approval. Since Zion's Hope Primitive Baptist Church is small, I told Hannah it might be better to use some funeral parlor. What do you think?"

"I think that would be best. I doubt if Dad believed in any church so we wouldn't be going against his wishes. Aunt Laura and Uncle Jess's funerals were at Blue Ridge Funeral Home on the road to Sophia and I thought their funerals were well conducted,"

Sarah looked at Hannah. "Is that all right with you Hannah?"

"I'd forgotten, but that was a nice funeral home and the proprietor treated us really well. We'll just have his funeral there, then," said Hannah with a sigh of relief.

"Do you want to bury him at that little cemetery over on the farm? If you do, we'll have to try to find somebody to dig the grave unless the funeral home has people to do that." Sarah looked at Freddie who grimaced.

"No! Dad hated the farm. If it hadn't been for Mom it would have been sold long ago. So, let's not bury him over there, Mom."

Hannah squeezed Freddie's hand. "You're right. Somehow it just wouldn't seem right. He really did hate the farm. I'll try to get a plot in one of the large cemeteries in the area."

"Mom, you really shouldn't have tried to come down here today. You're too weak."

The door behind them opened and Sergeant Keith McCauley came in. He stopped in surprise. "Well, you look like a happy man, Freddie."

Freddie turned a worried face toward him. "I'm happy to see Mom, but she shouldn't have come. Tell her how good I'm being treated, Keith."

"He is treated well, Mrs. Larkin. I've just brought him some books and snacks, see." Keith held out a bag, which he opened to reveal his gifts.

Hannah looked up at him and frowned. "Thanks, Sergeant, but don't you think your time would be better spent in trying to get him released?"

Keith gasped and Freddie stepped in. "Mom, Keith can't do things like that. He'd lose his job. My lawyer is out of town, but he will be here on Thursday and he'll get to work on getting me out on bail."

Keith looked so embarrassed that Sarah spoke up. "Hannah didn't mean to upset you. She's just so troubled over Freddie and can't seem to get anything done. She hadn't really recovered from her hospital stay when all this happened."

"That's all right. I understand how she feels. Can I be of any help?"

Freddie looked at his mother who was trembling all over and then looked at Keith. "Yes, Keith, please help Aunt Sarah get Mom back to the car, and Mom, don't worry about the funeral. I will go along with anything you decide. Right now, you need to go home and lie down."

Sarah smiled at Freddie. "Thank you, Freddie. She shouldn't have come, but she wanted to see you so much." Sarah grasped Hannah's arm.

"Come on, Hannah. Tell Freddie bye and then I'll get you to the car."

Hannah put her other hand through the slot and patted Freddie's hand and tried to squeeze it. "Bye, Freddie. I love you, Son."

"I know you do, Mom, and I love you, too. I'll be all right if you are taken care of so let Keith help you and Aunt Sarah to the car."

Keith grasped her other arm and she walked out of the room between them as Freddie turned away from the window.

She didn't like to have to accept any help from Keith McCauley, but right now she had no choice. She was almost as weak as she had been when she first came out of the hospital. *I wonder if stress and nerves caused this*, she thought as she tried to control her trembling.

CHAPTER 8

KEITH STOOD BY THE OPEN DOOR after seating Hannah in the car and still felt the animosity coming from her. He sighed inwardly before saying, "I think you should do as Freddie asked. He worries about you all the time."

Hannah didn't say anything, but Sarah said, "Thank you, Sergeant. I'll take her home and see that she rests. Do you know anything about whether they have finished with the autopsy? We haven't heard anything. That's why we haven't made arrangements."

Keith shook his head. "I'm sorry. I don't know, but I'll see if I can find out something and let you know. Drive carefully."

The car pulled out and soon was out of sight. Just then Steve Hammer came out and Keith went with him to a patrol car parked at the curb.

The two officers had just previously left the Henson home and they weren't very happy; they had too much to think about.

They had finished their interview with Sam and Martha Henson and returned to headquarters. Steve Hammer had gone in to report to the chief while Keith had checked on Freddie. Steve now turned to Sergeant McCauley.

"Sam Henson was certainly surprised that a special investigator was on the case. He's covering up something. I'd stake my twenty years of service on it."

"Who did call you in, Steve? I don't believe the chief did because he doesn't seem to want much delving for details. I think he would just as soon pin this on that boy, but I feel certain Freddie Larkin is innocent."

Steve Hammer didn't answer immediately but finally turned to Keith. "Let's just say, somebody with a lot of clout called the main office. The federal prosecutor called me, and after the interview I've just had, I'm pretty sure it wasn't the chief." He looked at Keith and grinned before Keith pulled out.

"At first I didn't want to come, but after I heard more of the details, I figured that somebody higher up wanted a quick arrest made. That caught my interest as being something not quite right."

"The chief wanted Freddie picked up after learning that he had already been arrested once for drug use. From there I knew that with a little digging they'd found that he and Sam Henson's daughter had spent the night in jail. So, I'm thinking somebody thought they'd found their patsy," said Keith with a furrowed brow.

"Oh yeah, it's getting clearer. I can see the whole picture. When questioned, the Henson girl blurted out that Freddie Larkin had done drugs because he hated his dad. That and his fingerprints on the glass were all that the chief needed to issue an arrest warrant," replied Steve.

"Well, he has a good lawyer, and I feel sure that Freddie will be released soon. I just hope his lawyer has some good investigators working for him," said Sergeant McCauley. "His mother is too frail to stand much more."

Steve gave Keith a narrow-eyed look, as he remembered how careful Keith was in the presence of Mrs. Larkin. He shrugged.

"We've talked to two people but several more are tangled up in this mess. Thomas Mitchell may as well be the next one."

"I don't know of any connection he has with this case except that he is the Vice President of CEE," said the sergeant.

"That and the fact that he has been seen with Sabrina Draper on several occasions in very intimate settings," Steve smirked.

Sergeant McCauley's eyebrows went up. "Thomas Mitchell? Are you sure?"

"You want pictures? That woman has been watched for quite some time now. She definitely gets around," replied Steve.

Sergeant McCauley drove slowly back toward the entrance of Robert C. Byrd Drive without commenting. He suddenly looked at his watch. "It's almost time for supper. Do you want to go by Long John's and get something to eat?"

Steve agreed and they were soon pulling into the parking lot. When they had parked, McCauley stepped out of the car and almost bumped into Margie Meadows.

"Excuse me, Ma'am. Did I hurt you?" he asked as he suddenly recognized James Harrison's secretary.

Margie smiled and started to ease by him when he said, "I almost didn't recognize you. You're James Harrison's secretary, aren't you?"

Startled, Margie stammered. "Yes . . . Yes, I am. How do you know me?"

"I came up to see Mr. Harrison about the fundraising we were doing for 'Toys for Tots' last Christmas. I guess you were too busy to notice me."

Margie smiled. "I guess that's the case, Sergeant. Excuse me, please." She eased between the cars on her way into the restaurant. She didn't notice Steve Hammer on the other side of the car.

"There goes a really nice lady," Steve said, watching Margie walk toward the restaurant.

"How do you know her?" asked Sergeant McCauley as they too walked to the restaurant.

"I was introduced to her at a birthday party twenty years ago, in the state of Washington. Small world, isn't it? I've never forgotten her and have tried to catch up to her and get acquainted since then, but she is elusive. I've asked about her and have been given glowing accounts of what a kind, and caring lady she is," replied Steve.

They entered the restaurant and took a seat in the aisle near the windows. As they sat waiting they scanned the restaurant. "Remember our conversation about Thomas Mitchell? Don't look now, but three seats behind you is Mitchell with Sabrina Draper," Steve Hammer said in a muted voice.

Sergeant McCauley rose from his seat. "I need to wash my hands, so make sure the server brings me unsweetened tea." He turned and started up the aisle to stop as if surprised.

"Mr. Mitchell, how are you? And Miss, uh Draper, isn't it? I'm glad I ran into the both of you. When we have finished eating, could we go some place and talk?" asked Sergeant McCauley.

Sabrina blanched, but Mitchell smiled and calmly said, "I'm at your disposal, but I don't know about Miss Draper."

Sabrina gulped and said, "Sure, it's all right with me." Then she asked, "Where do you want to meet? My office is just down the street, and nobody is there today."

Sergeant McCauley nodded. "Thanks. That will be fine."

Meanwhile, Margie Meadows had hurried away from her brief encounter with Sergeant Keith McCauley and the older man who was with him in the restaurant. As she went out the door recognition dawned, *I met that man in the state of Washington. What is he doing way out here? Is he following me?* She thought as she pulled into the CEE parking lot.

Riding up in the elevator she kept the man's face on her mind and knew that he had asked several people about her after she'd met him at a birthday party. She had also had three calls from numbers she did not recognize and had not returned the calls. This made her very uneasy, but she tried to put it out of her mind. She knew she hadn't done anything in Washington that needed investigating or watching so she decided to forget it.

"Right now, I need to call Hannah. No, I'd better say Mrs. Larkin since she doesn't know me. I know all about her though." Margie was talking aloud since she knew the office was empty.

She picked up the phone and dialed Hannah's number. Sarah answered. "Sarah, how is Mrs. Larkin this evening? I know you took her to see Freddie today."

"She's tired and weak, but she held up pretty good until right there at the last few minutes."

"What happened to cause that?"

"Nothing except Sergeant McCauley came in and she got upset with him for not getting Freddie out. He couldn't, of course, but I guess she needed to hit out at somebody and the sergeant seems to be the one she hits, if he's around. Anyway, Freddie asked McCauley to help me get her to the car and told Hannah that she shouldn't blame the sergeant."

Margie smiled since she suspected that the sergeant was struck by Hannah's beauty. "Why doesn't she like him? I know he was the one who arrested Freddie, but the chief sent him to do that."

"I know, Miss, uh Margie, but somehow, in Hannah's mind Sergeant McCauley is all tied up with Bill's death and Freddie's arrest. I think when Freddie gets out she'll be all right.

Margie smiled at the phone. "Do you think she feels well enough to have some company this evening?" she asked on impulse.

"She'd love to have you visit. She's all the time telling me how you came to comfort her when Freddie was arrested. I certainly thank you for that. Hannah said she felt like she did when her mother comforted her when she was a girl," replied Sarah.

"Well, I'll come and play mother again. What if I stop by Long John's and bring us all some fish for dinner? Do you think that will be all right?" asked Margie.

Sarah was smiling, and Margie could hear it in her voice. "Great! I might even talk to you if you bring fish."

Margie suddenly remembered that she'd already bought fish for her own supper. *I'll just go back and get some more*, she thought. She hung up the phone feeling the best she had in almost forty years.

Sarah thought about how good Sergeant Keith McCauley was being to Freddie. She knew that was unusual and McCauley had also come to see how Hannah was getting along several times. In fact, Keith McCauley had offered to drive Hannah to see Freddie, but as it turned out she had driven Hannah to see Freddie herself and now Margie was coming to visit. Sarah put the phone down with a big smile on her face.

As Margie got ready to leave her office before going to Long John Silver's she thought, *McCauley seems like such a nice man, but all men seem nice until they get what they want. I just don't know what his motives are where Hannah is concerned.*

She shook her head in determination. "I'm not going to let my suspicions spoil my evening with Hannah. This may be the only chance I'll have to spend an entire evening with her." She mumbled quietly as she straightened her desk, and made sure that all the cabinets were locked. Then taking her coat, she went out the door and locked it behind her.

Mr. Harrison had impressed upon her from the beginning to always keep everything about the office under lock and key. She had set the pattern then, and for almost twenty-one years she had kept to it. She thought too much of James Harrison to do otherwise.

I don't know if I love him or not. Well, I do love him, but I don't know if it's just appreciation for his kindness or what it is. I just know that I love him. I'll never know anymore than that either, even if he does respect me enough to think I'm good enough to marry. That must mean that he likes me and trusts me, but he's never asked me out or in any way seemed interested in me as a woman, thought Margie sadly. Margie knew she could trust James Harrison. He was the only man she had met in over thirty five years whom she would have dared to trust, except of course Bill Larkin. But that was a different story, one that hadn't yet been told and might never be.

Margie grimaced and hurriedly left the building. Her eagerness to spend an entire evening with Hannah Larkin and Sarah Preston surpassed any other thoughts and she walked with a happy pace to her car.

She pulled into the Larkin driveway at six-thirty that evening. Almost all the way Margie had hummed a tune, except for the several minutes at a time she had spent recalling how kind and generous James Harrison had always been to her. She couldn't imagine another boss taking the time to put his own lawyer on a case just because his secretary expressed a need. These thoughts made her long for someone who really cared for her. She put that all in the back of her mind as she got out of the car with her purse and a heavy box of fish, coleslaw, hush puppies, and corn.

Sarah must have been watching for her since she was out the door and down the steps before Margie had closed the car door.

"You brought the fish. Does this mean you're trying to be Hannah's mother again?" asked Sarah, laughing as she took the box from her.

"Of course it does. Who else but a mother would work all day and then go buy fish for someone's supper," countered Margie, smiling broadly.

They were both laughing as they went through the door into the house. "Hannah, look what your mother brought us," called Sarah.

Hannah came out of the bathroom still drying her hair. She smiled at Margie. "This is exactly like a mother; or at least like my mother was. You're not old enough to be my mother though, so I guess you'll just have to be mother of our hearts."

Margie looked at Hannah with such a pleasant smile. "That's what makes you so pretty, Hannah. You're so nice and pretty on the inside and it shows on the outside."

Hannah smiled and wearily kept rubbing her hair. "My head would really swell if this heavy, wet hair didn't weigh it down."

"You certainly have beautiful hair, that's for sure - wet or not," said Margie as she started unloading the box.

"That's what Sergeant McCauley says," quipped Sarah bringing a frown to Hannah's face.

"Come and sit down, Hannah. We'll set out the plates and divide the food, said Margie.

CHAPTER 9

MCCAULEY AND HAMMER WERE STILL AT Long John's when Margie had met them earlier. They went in to eat and found that Thomas Mitchell and Sabrina Draper were also there. McCauley set up a meeting with them and then went to the bathroom. When he returned to his seat, he found Thomas Mitchell and Sabrina Draper's booth empty.

"They sure left in a hurry. What did you say to them?" asked Steve as Sergeant McCauley took his seat.

"I just asked them if we could talk to both of them. I think it shook the Draper woman up, but it didn't seem to have any effect on Thomas Mitchell," replied the sergeant.

After they had stopped by the cash register and paid their bill, Sergeant McCauley noticed that Steve was looking around.

"Can't you find Miss Meadows, Steve?" he asked with raised eyebrows.

Steve grinned and walked out the door, not speaking until they were outside. "I think she must have picked up an order and taken it away. I looked around while you were in the restroom, and she wasn't in the restaurant."

"You are really interested in her, aren't you?" said Keith. Steve Hammer was sixty and eligible to retire. He was also a man without a wife, like himself, and Keith suspected that he worked so much overtime because he was lonely.

"Well, she's nice looking, she's intelligent, and she isn't out chasing every man she sees. So yes, I'm interested," replied Steve as he fastened his seat belt.

Keith grinned and nodded in satisfaction. "That's good . . . Yes Sir-ee. I think that's just great."

Steve Hammer looked across at him with a frown. "I don't get your meaning. Why should my liking Margie Meadows matter to you."

"I'll tell you later, but right now let's go see if these next two pieces of the web have anything interesting to tell us." Keith backed the patrol car up and turned toward the exit.

They didn't have far to go, which didn't give them any time to discuss what information they needed from either Thomas Mitchell or Sabrina Draper. Keith mentioned this as they arrived.

"We're going in without an agenda. Maybe that Draper woman will get nervous and tell us something that will solve the case," said Keith.

"You wish? I certainly hope she does, but it isn't likely," replied Steve as they pulled into the parking lot located by the side of the office building.

They took the stairs to the second floor and commented about the nice facilities some people had to work in. "The way this corporation is set up is strange. Mr. Harrison and Mr. Mitchell have offices in the Doorn Building on Robert C. Byrd Drive, Sam Henson has his office across town in one of his own buildings, and this building houses what was Larkin's domain," explained Steve as they arrived on the second floor landing.

They didn't know what had taken place from the time Sabrina Draper and Thomas Mitchell had left Long John's, but later Thomas Mitchell filled them in.

According to Mitchell, Sabrina Draper had nearly fainted when Sergeant McCauley had approached her table. When he left she'd said to Thomas, "I've got to get out of here. Let's go."

Thomas resisted. "I have nothing to hide. Have you?" he asked.

"No and yes," she murmured as she rose from her seat.

Thomas shrugged, but stood also. He hadn't as yet gotten the information he wanted from Sabrina. He followed her, stopping long enough to pay the tab.

They were soon pulling into the parking space behind Sabrina's office. Now she was trembling so badly that Thomas became concerned.

"Sabrina, you need to pull yourself together. You say you didn't kill Bill, so why are you so upset?"

Sabrina didn't say anything until they were out of the car and in the elevator. "Thomas, I gave Bill two bottles of Mylanta, but I swear they were given to me at that conference on stress management. That's why I said yes and no."

The elevator stopped at the second floor. They exited and walked down the hall, passing Bill's office on the way. When Sabrina saw the wreath of flowers on the door, she stopped.

"Where did that come from? Does CEE do this when an employee dies?" asked Sabrina.

"I don't think we've had a death before." He reached over and pulled out a piece of paper he had seen sticking from the center of the wreath. Sabrina stepped closer to see the writing on it. It was printed in bold print with a Sharpie and had the following message:

"YOUR SINS WILL FIND YOU OUT AND YOU WILL REAP WHAT YOU SOW SO WATCH YOUR STEP"

Sabrina gasped and stepped back. Thomas started to put the paper in his pocket, but instead put it back in the center of the wreath in such a way that it would be seen.

Sabrina turned and tried to put her key in the lock. She was shaking so badly that Thomas took the key from her and opened the door.

When they were in and the door was shut, Sabrina blurted, "I need some cocaine. I won't be able to talk to that cop in the shape I'm in."

Thomas looked at her in surprise. "I hope you don't think I have cocaine on me. I don't use the stuff."

"No, I know you don't, but I do have some. I was just warning you before I used it," she replied as she quickly went into her bathroom and closed the door.

Not wanting to be caught where cocaine was being used, Thomas walked close to the door and said loudly, "You'd better hurry and get rid of it before Sergeant McCauley gets here. I wouldn't have come if I'd known you were planning to do this."

Thomas stood pacing around the room and had started toward the door when Sabrina came out. "Don't worry. There's nothing left in there, not even an odor. Check it for yourself."

Thomas walked over to the bathroom door and looked in. Nothing was out of place and the room smelled of lavender. He relaxed and came back to sit in a chair pulled up in the front of her desk.

"Who knows that you gave the Mylanta to Bill Larkin?" asked Thomas curiously.

Sabrina pulled in a long breath. "His wife knew because she called the police and told them. His son also knew, but I don't know if Bill told them or what. I wish I'd never met Bill

Larkin. I wouldn't have if Sam Henson hadn't given me that big raise to be Bill's assistant."

Thomas sat quietly, taking all this in. He thought, *Sam Henson hasn't said anything about giving Sabrina Draper a big raise. He had to hide it in some other expense. I have been going over his accounts and there was certainly no mention of Sabrina.*

"Who did you say gave you the Mylanta?" asked Thomas.

"Margie Meadows handed it out. She gave everybody that wanted it, two bottles each. So there couldn't have been anything wrong with the Mylanta or somebody else would have reported being sick by now, wouldn't they?" asked Sabrina worriedly.

Thomas didn't have time to answer, since McCauley and Hammer were walking down the hall. At their first knock on the door Thomas Mitchell opened it and across the room Sabrina Draper was sitting almost as motionless as a still life painting. Thomas, stepped aside and offered the two men seats.

"You two left before you finished your lunch didn't you?" asked Steve Hammer giving Sabrina a keen look.

Thomas grinned. "I did, that's for sure. They had grilled salmon today and it was delicious. I thought about asking for a doggie bag before we left."

Sabrina saw that Thomas had thrown her under the bus. "The chicken I ordered made me nauseous. I asked Thomas to leave."

"I never order chicken anywhere. My grandmother got food poisoning from eating chicken and dumplings at a church dinner and I've been afraid of it ever since," said Sergeant McCauley, also looking narrowly at Sabrina.

"Do you feel well enough to talk now, Miss Draper?" Steve asked.

When Sabrina raised her head and Steve got a good look at her eyes, he knew immediately that she had used some kind of stimulant. Her eyes were shining as if they had been polished. She smiled as she said, "Sure. What do you wish to talk about?"

"I understand that you gave Bill Larkin two bottles of Mylanta, and what he drank from one of those bottles was laced with a large amount of cyanide poison. Where did you get the poison, Miss Draper?" asked Steve as if he knew she had put it in the Mylanta.

Sabrina gasped. Her eyes widened. She gulped for air, coughed several times, but finally blurted. "I don't know . . . I mean I don't know anything about poison. I certainly did not have any poison, nor did I put any in that Mylanta. Margie Meadows gave me two bottles already in a brown paper bag and I brought it back home . . . uh, back to the office, and gave it to Bill. He had been having trouble with his stomach and had told me that both he and his wife had been taking Mylanta.

Keith McCauley's eyes widened and he quickly asked, "Do you know who supplied the Mylanta to the conference?"

"No, and I didn't ask. I thought that some pharmaceutical company gave it out since the conference was on stress management," explained Sabrina.

Steve Hammer turned to Mitchell. "You are Executive Vice President of CEE?"

Thomas replied in the affirmative and Steve then asked, "Who in your corporation usually gets contributions such as Mylanta, toothpaste, or whatever to hand out at these conferences?"

Thomas thought for a few seconds. "You know, I think Sam Henson mostly does that, but I can't say for certain that this was something he did. I mean it could have been somebody from another project."

"Do you ever bring in contributions of this sort, Mr. Mitchell?" asked Sergeant McCauley.

"No, I never have, but that is mostly because I only look at the business plans, the prospectus, and other start-up data once it has been reviewed by someone like Bill Larkin," answered Thomas.

"How well did you know Bill Larkin, Mr. Mitchell?" asked Steve Hammer.

"I knew his business acumen better than I knew the man. He was a stickler for detail, accuracy, and honesty," answered Thomas.

Sergeant McCauley suddenly turned back to Sabrina. "How about you, Miss Draper? How well did you know Bill Larkin?"

Sabrina turned white, gulped, and slumped forward toward the floor. McCauley caught her just before she landed.

"Call the rescue squad, Steve," he ordered as he lifted Sabrina onto the leather sofa against the wall.

"Was she really already sick or was this because of something else?" McCauley asked somewhat suspiciously.

"I think she needs to answer that, Sergeant," said Thomas since he did not want to become involved in this case unless he was forced to.

When the rescue team arrived and began to check Sabrina, the EMT looked up and said, "Has she taken anything recently? Any pain medicine or anything like that?"

Hammer and McCauley both turned to look at Thomas Mitchell. "How much should I tell them?" wondered Thomas as he braced for their questions.

"Mr. Mitchell, Miss Draper told us she felt sick after she ate chicken at Long John Silver's. Was she still sick when you both arrived here?" Steve Hammer asked.

"She was trembling so badly that I had to take her key and unlock the door. She went straight to the bathroom and stayed in there a few minutes. But she seemed fine when she came out," replied Thomas.

McCauley pursed his lips as if deciding something. He turned to the EMT. "How is the young lady?"

"Her heart rate is up and her pulse is rapid. We're taking her to the hospital," answered the EMT just as a gurney was set up. Sabrina was loaded onto it and wheeled out of the office and down the hall to the elevator.

Hammer, McCauley, and Mitchell all stepped into the hall as if checking to make sure they were really taking her away. As the elevator door closed, the three men turned back into the office and wandered aimlessly until Steve Hammer bent over behind Sabrina's desk. When he straightened back up, he held Sabrina's purse in his hand.

"We'll have to take this to the hospital. I'm sure they will need to see her insurance information and identification. She may even have medication that she carries with her. I'm surprised they didn't look for things like that before they left."

McCauley took the purse and opened it. "You two are witnesses that I am only looking for medications, insurance, and identification," he said as he began emptying the purse and placing it on the desk. When he unzipped a small pocket, he pulled out a plastic bag with some white powder in it. "What have we here?"

Steve Hammer looked at Thomas, then at McCauley. "In case either of you haven't seen cocaine before, this is cocaine," he said holding the bag out for them to see. "I suspected she'd used it when we came in. Her eyes looked like glittering ice."

Both men looked at Mitchell. "Did you know she had this?"

Thomas thought he may as well tell them, since they'd found it anyway. "I didn't know where she had it, but when we came back here she was in a state. She said she had to have some cocaine in order to talk to you. I told her I didn't do drugs and wanted no part of it. She went into the bathroom and stayed a few minutes. When she came out she was much calmer. I assumed she had it hidden in the bathroom," answered Thomas.

"Man, this web is getting more tangled by the minute. Are you also hiding something, Mr. Mitchell?" asked Sergeant McCauley.

Thomas grimaced. "Now listen here. I do not do drugs. I didn't know she had any, and I'm not trying to hide anything."

"Are you having an affair with Miss Draper? I know that you have been out with her several times," Steve Hammer said.

"I've had dinner with her a few times, but that's it. My dealings with Miss Draper are all purely professional," answered Thomas, bristling.

"Mr. Mitchell, you are both working for the same company, so what kind of business would require a candlelight dinner? I wasn't born yesterday," snapped Hammer.

"Regardless of what you believe, I am not having an affair with Miss Draper. I refuse to answer further questions without my attorney," stated Thomas, giving Steve an angry look.

Suddenly Steve pulled a slip of paper from his pocket. "What do you know about this?" He produced the printed message from the wreath of flowers on Bill Larkin's door.

"I know what you know. We found it when we passed Larkin's office and read the message. It frightened Miss Draper, so I put it back in the wreath and we came here," said Thomas. "If you have further questions I'd like to call my attorney."

"That's all right, Mr. Mitchell. You can go on home or wherever you planned to go. If we need you, we will be back in touch and you can call all the attorneys you wish," said McCauley as he began picking up the contents of Sabrina's purse.

Thomas glared at each of them before he walked out of the office and down the hall. As soon as the door closed behind him, Keith said, "Steve we need to get this purse to the hospital, but since it is on the way let's stop by and see Hannah and Margie first."

"Okay, but we'll need to lock this purse in the trunk of your car. We sure don't want to lose this piece of evidence."

CHAPTER 10

BACK AT THE LARKIN RESIDENCE, SARAH, Margie, and Hannah were ready to sit down at the table when the doorbell rang and Sarah went to answer it. Soon she stepped back through the door. "We have company. Sergeant McCauley and Inspector Hammer have come to visit."

Margie and Hannah both turned and Margie stopped filling the plate she held in her hand and sat waiting as if suspended in time.

"Hello, Sergeant," said Hannah. "This is Margie Meadows, our good friend."

Margie smiled. "I know Keith McCauley, Hannah, but I don't think I know his friend. You look familiar, though," she said looking toward Steve Hammer.

Steve smiled. "I was introduced to you at a birthday party a good while ago, but I don't think you were very impressed."

"I hope I wasn't rude. I don't meet new people, easily," replied Margie stiffly.

Sarah sniffed. "Margie brought fish from Long John's for dinner tonight. It looks as if there's plenty, so you two join us. That's all right, isn't it, Margie?" asked Sarah, laughing at the looks she received from Margie and Hannah.

Margie laughed. "Sure, if Hannah doesn't mind, I don't." When Hannah nodded, she smiled.

Both men held up their hands. They smiled and rubbed their stomachs. "We just ate supper at Long John's. In fact I almost knocked Miss Meadows down when we parked," said Keith, smiling at Margie.

Margie's eyes widened. "That's right, you did. I was parked right beside you. Anyway, you're both welcome if you're still hungry.

Steve smiled. "Thanks, but not this time. I'm stuffed."

"Well, as long as you know you're welcome. After all, how many cops do we know that come calling in the home of a hardened criminal like Freddie Larkin as well as treat him almost like a son?" asked Margie, looking at Keith.

Hannah was still not sure if she liked him, and gave him a narrow-eyed look of inspection. "Freddie says I need to thank you, sergeant, so I suppose you are being good to him."

With all that damp hair curling around her elfin face and her soft brown eyes looking so sad, she brought out the protective instinct in Keith, but he could do nothing about it.

He smiled. "I felt like Freddie was innocent and still do. You both have been through a lot and still have more before you. I want you to know that I'll be here if you need me, either of you," stated Keith seriously.

Hannah had trouble in even being polite, but she tried to smile her thanks. She turned to Steve Hammer. "Do you work with Sergeant McCauley all the time?"

"I've been working with him on this case. It's worse than a spider's web. A web stays mostly in one place, but this thing is all over the place,"

Steve looked embarrassed as he realized the things that had recently happened to Hannah. Her husband had been murdered eight days before and hadn't yet been buried, due to the delay in the autopsy. Her son had been arrested as well and here she was trying to entertain people.

Steve knew that the services of James Harrison's lawyer, Jerome Judson, had been acquired by Margie for this case. Judson's man had visited Freddie and asked Chief Donaldson to rush up the arraignment so he could get bail for Freddie. Even though the chief didn't seem to like the idea, Steve knew that he couldn't stall much longer.

Since Keith McCauley was so interested in Hannah's welfare he was glad that a lawyer like Judson was on the case. He also felt that working closely with Steve, a federal investigator, would be helpful in solving the case. Keith smiled at Steve, but kept his thoughts to himself.

Margie felt that Freddie was innocent and needed to be home to help Hannah and she had expressed this to both Steve and Keith. They had talked about the trauma Hannah had faced finding her husband dead and then her son being arrested. Hannah wasn't very large anyway and now she looked like a big puff of wind could blow her away.

Sarah filled her plate and sat down at the table. "Sergeant, what's taking them so long on the autopsy? This waiting is getting Hannah down and to tell the truth it isn't easy on me either."

Keith answered. "I don't know, Mrs. Preston. Do you know anything about it, Steve?" Keith looked at Hannah and noted her pallor. He hoped this would soon be over for her.

Steve added. "You know, I haven't asked. They are taking an inordinate amount of time, though. I'll drop by the pathology lab tomorrow and see what I can find out."

ADDA LEAH DAVIS

While the women were eating and the men both had cokes, Steve looked first at Hannah and then Margie and smiled. "I'm glad we have finally met, Miss Meadows. I've thought about calling Mr. Harrison's office several times, but couldn't muster the nerve to do it."

"Why would you need to call me?" asked Margie. She stopped with her fork in the air as if puzzled.

Steve took a seat beside Keith. His face was red, and when he didn't answer Keith did.

"Miss Meadows, this man would like to get to know you better. He's a great investigator but pretty bad in social situations," Keith said, looking sideways at Steve.

Now Margie's face was red and Sarah turned her head to hide her laughter. "Hannah, look at your adopted mother. What's your answer, Margie?" asked Sarah, smiling broadly.

Margie snapped. "My . . . . The head of this house is lying dead in a morgue, and the family is in need of support. This is not the time to talk about getting to know me, Mr. Hammer."

Steve's face turned red and his eyes widened. "I didn't mean right now, Miss Meadows." Then in a humbler voice he said, "I had planned to wait until all this is over if you will consider it."

Margie hesitated for a moment and then looked steadily at Steve. "We'll talk after all of this is over. You may change your mind. You don't know me, and I don't know you. As far as you know, I may be the one you're looking for."

Every head turned with startled gasps. Margie turned a mottled red color, but tried to smile. "I couldn't get a soul to sell me any poison, though."

Hannah smiled. "You couldn't hurt anybody if you tried."

Margie got up and put her arms around Hannah. "Don't I have a sweet daughter-in…I mean daughter?"

Keith McCauley smiled widely. "Indeed, you do, Miss Meadows."

Sarah did laugh this time. "Now, Hannah's face is red. Somebody say something nice about me, so these other two women won't be so embarrassed."

There was an uneasy silence until Steve said, "We'd best get out of here, Keith. We've come at the wrong time and won't be welcome much longer."

He turned to Sarah, "I'll check on the autopsy, Mrs. Preston, and let you know."

Both men started for the door, but Keith turned. "I'm sorry. We've acted like uncaring idiots. We've been way out of line and the only excuse we have is that we rarely meet real ladies. We aren't usually this uncouth so if you ladies should need any help please give us a call."

Back in the car they drove in silence until Steve said, "We sure goofed, didn't we?"

Keith shook his head. "We sure did. We'd better just stick to law enforcement."

Soon, they had the case back on their minds. When they started talking about Thomas Mitchell, Steve turned to Keith with a puzzled expression.

"He's one cool dude, isn't he?"

Keith remained silent for a minute. "Yes, he is, but I believe he told the truth and I don't believe he is into drugs."

"I'd love to know what Margie Meadows thinks of Thomas Mitchell, wouldn't you, Keith?"

"I'd love to ask her about everybody that works for CEE. I'll bet she knows a lot about most of them, especially those in the upper echelons," answered Keith.

"Your precious little Hannah would breathe a lot easier if she knew what we've just discovered, wouldn't she?" Steve looked speculatively at Keith.

Keith looked at Steve. "I hope it doesn't show, but I had put women out of my life completely until I met Hannah Larkin. When I arrived and saw her on her knees lying over the body of her husband I felt like grabbing her up and running away with her."

Steve grinned. "You've got it bad, but we can't tell her anything so watch your step."

"I'm not crazy. My heart is touched, but not my brain. So, let's get back on the case," said Keith.

They decided to go back to Bill Larkin's office and see if there was any evidence left there. Going up the stairs they still discussed the case.

"Well, Mitchell may not have used cocaine or knew anything about it, but he's uneasy about something," said Steve as they went in the door. He strode across the room and bent to pull out desk drawers. "Locked tight," he said as he tugged at the bottom drawer. "Oh ho! One unlocked drawer! Let's see what we have here."

The drawer was empty except for a pair of felt house slippers. He then tried each drawer of the row of file cabinets. They were locked as well.

"I think we'd better hurry and get Miss Draper's purse to the hospital, don't you?" asked Steve.

"Yes, a patrol car trunk is usually safe, but I'd rather have that purse in a safer place. Do you think Miss Draper got food poisoning, or was she overwrought for fear we'd find something?" Keith asked.

Steve rolled his eyes and ran his hand through his hair. "Every bit of this has something to do with the workings of this corporation, but I don't know what it is. Freddie Larkin was arrested, but I think he has less to do with all this than any one we've talked to. I could be wrong, though, because the boy did go wild for a few years."

After one last survey of the office, they turned the lights off and left the office, locking the door behind them.

Soon they were at the hospital, and after showing their badges they asked to see the doctor treating Sabrina Draper. They were sent to ICU. They stopped a nurse and asked about the case, and soon a doctor appeared.

Steve Hammer stepped forward. "Doctor, we brought Miss Draper's purse along, since we felt you would need insurance and other pertinent information."

Sergeant McCauley displayed his badge and introduced himself and then turned to Hammer. "This brash fellow is one of those 'super-smart' federal investigators and he and I were present when Miss Draper passed out."

The doctor put out his hand. "I'm Doctor Zimmer, and I do appreciate you bringing this to us. If you will come with me, we can go over what we have learned so far."

They were soon in a well-appointed office, seated in front of a large desk. "Do you know if Miss Draper has relatives living near, or anywhere for that matter? There are some things that her family should know. Being police, you will have to be informed also."

Steve spoke up. "Are you trying to tell us that Miss Draper had used cocaine shortly before we met with her? We already know that, or at least we suspect she had. We found a bag of what we suspect is cocaine in her purse."

"Good. We'll have to check that, because we not only found cocaine- we also found poison in her system," stated the doctor.

"Poison!" gasped both men almost simultaneously and then turned to look at each other.

"Doctor, we are investigating the murder of Bill Larkin, who was employed by Civic Enterprise Endeavors. He was poisoned, and now you tell us that Miss Draper was as well. She works there too."

"How is Miss Draper? We need to talk to her," said Hammer.

"She's going to be all right, physically, I think, but you can't talk to her today. Check back tomorrow afternoon, and if she is stable, she may be able to talk," said Dr. Zimmer.

"We'll need to post a guard on her room. If someone sold, or gave her poisoned cocaine, she is in a very precarious position," stated Hammer.

The doctor agreed and said that they would refuse admission to anyone except the police. Sergeant McCauley put in several calls to the station and also asked to speak to the chief. When he answered, McCauley gave a brief account and the chief said, "You'll have to pick Thomas Mitchell up on suspicion, since he was with her and knew about the cocaine. He may have been in on it. I don't give a damn whether he gets a lawyer or not, you still have to bring him down to the station."

"I guess you want us to wait until the morning, don't you?" Keith rolled his eyes at Steve and held the phone out enough for Steve to hear.

"Hell, yes, I want you to wait until the morning. I can't work this damn job all day and all night too, and I want to be in on the questioning of mister 'high and mighty' Mitchell."

CHAPTER 11

MEANWHILE IN THE LARKIN HOUSEHOLD, SARAH and Margie were cleaning up the kitchen. They had insisted that Hannah lie down but she still cleared the table, folded the table cloth, and put it away before she left.

Margie looked at Sarah for a moment then drew in a long breath. "Sarah, how long have you known Hannah and Bill?"

Sarah grinned. "When they first moved here, about twenty years ago, I was part of the welcoming committee that came to visit them."

"Did . . . had Freddie already been born?"

"No, they lived here about six months before Hannah got pregnant." Sarah laughed. "If her Aunt Laura hadn't asked her if she was pregnant I don't know when she would have found out. They were both surprised."

Margie rinsed her dish cloth and hung it on the sink. "Bill seemed like such a fine man, but I didn't know him personally."

"He was . . . or at least I thought he was, until he started working on that Blennoc Project and had to take that Draper woman as his assistant."

Margie's ears perked up. "Did he change then?"

"He sure did. He wouldn't speak to Hannah half the time, he took the check book and only gave her a small allowance, and he started staying away nights and weekends. I think he was sleeping with that Draper woman, but Hannah has never even thought such a thing."

They were ready to go to the living room when the phone rang. Sarah picked it up. "Hello! This is Sarah Preston speaking. Yes, it is. I'm a friend of Mrs. Larkin. I'll take the phone to her. She isn't well."

Sarah went to Hannah. "This is the morgue, Hannah. Their autopsy is complete and they need to know where you want Bill's . . . Bill sent. What funeral home?"

Seeing Hannah's shocked look, Margie said, "Ask if we can call back and get the number."

Sarah soon hung up the phone and turned toward Hannah who was sitting transfixed or so it seemed. She didn't speak until Margie spoke and broke the spell.

"What about Durgins? You may have some other place in mind, but it's pretty convenient." Margie sat down beside Hannah and waited.

Hannah shook her head as if to clear her thoughts. The reality of the words 'funeral home' hit her like a shock wave of emotion. *This is real and Bill, my husband, is being discussed and he has no say in our decision*, she thought. After a moment Hannah spoke.

"I'm trying to think of the name of that place where they had Uncle Jess and Aunt Laura. Freddie told us, Sarah, when we visited him. I think it was on Route 54. Do you remember the name, Sarah?"

"It was the Blue Ridge Funeral Home. It's on Robert C. Byrd Drive on the road toward Sophia," said Sarah.

Hannah took a deep breath and tried to be more in control. "I can't understand why I couldn't remember that. We were there twice in two years, weren't we?"

Sarah looked at Margie. "What she means is that her Uncle Jess died one year and her Aunt Laura just seemed to give up and she died the next year. They really loved each other."

At the sound of a muffled sob, they both turned toward Hannah as she made her way out of the room toward the bathroom.

"Margie, I'm so worried about Hannah. Somebody almost killed her, too. I can't prove it. Not yet anyway. She's only been out of the hospital about a month. She had poison in her system also," related Sarah.

Margie gasped. "How do you know that? Did the doctor tell you?"

Sarah sat very still. "The doctor said Hannah had a lot of inflammation in her stomach and someone told Freddie that poison had been found in her system. Freddie didn't tell me who told him, but someone saw her hospital records and saw that it was noted that poison had been found in her system. She was bleeding and she also had been taking Mylanta. We both know that Mylanta is really good for an upset stomach, but it didn't help her. She almost died, Margie, and she hadn't gained her strength back when this all happened."

Margie sat in a deep study. She couldn't believe that someone wanted Bill Larkin out of the way that much. It seemed as if they tried to murder his wife and put the blame on him.

"Sarah, did Freddie tell Keith McCauley about his mother being poisoned?"

"No, I don't think he did, or if he did he hadn't at the time he told me."

"Somebody needs to know and if anybody can get to the bottom of this, Keith McCauley can. He's a very honest man, and I believe you can trust him."

Sarah made no reply because Hannah came back into the room just then.

"I guess I'd better call the morgue . . ." Hannah stopped and furiously swiped her hand across her face. "I hate tears. They don't help a thing . . . they just make a person look awful and feel worse."

Margie jumped up. "Hannah, we told them we would call back. We can wait until you have decided."

Hannah looked at Margie. "Sarah and I talked about this and Sarah thought we should take him to a funeral home since it is more convenient and larger than the little church Freddie and I attend. Freddie agreed the day Sarah and I visited him."

Sarah had been sitting quietly. "Hannah, I remember those people at Blue Ridge Funeral Home being really nice. I think that's a good place to send Bill's body."

Margie came over and sat beside Hannah. "If that's the facility you want then that's who we'll get. We don't want you worrying so if you don't mind, Sarah and I will make all the funeral arrangements, won't we, Sarah?"

"I'll turn the television on," said Margie as she adjusted a pillow on the sofa. "Why don't you just lie back and rest while Sarah and I plan all this out."

Sarah and Margie went to the kitchen table and wrote out what they thought would be satisfactory with Hannah.

Margie brought it to her. "Look this over and see if everything is all right with you?"

Margie sat waiting to give Hannah time to read it. Sarah remained in the kitchen.

Hannah nodded wearily. "I can't believe this is real. I keep watching the street, thinking that Bill's headlights will shine through the window as they always used to when he came home late."

"It takes some time to adjust, Hannah, but you still have Freddie and he needs you very much," said Margie.

"I need him too, Miss Meadows. In fact, I don't know what I'd do right now without Freddie, Sarah, and you too. You're both like my guardian angels. I don't know how to thank either of you."

Margie sat with a pensive expression. "Well, right now you can tell us whether these arrangements are satisfactory and then Sarah can let the mortuary know what to do."

Hannah looked over the list and nodded. "I think everything is covered so go ahead and tell them to send Bill to the Blue Ridge Funeral Home."

Hannah was trembling again and Margie sat down by her on the sofa. "Hannah, I'm going to tell you what my doctor told me and it helped. I had something really bad happen to me when I first met this doctor. I was in about the same shape you're in and the doctor said to go ahead and cry for a while, but one morning I would wake up and realize that I couldn't change the past, but I could change what happened in the future. His advice was to get up each morning determined to do something good with my day."

Hannah had been watching Margie as she talked. "Miss . . . May I call you Margie?"

"Nothing would please me more," said Margie, blinking her eyes rapidly and turning her head to the side.

"I feel like you've overcome something bad in your life. Have you, Margie?" asked Hannah.

Margie looked at Hannah speculatively. "Yes, Hannah, I have. I'll tell you about it sometime."

Sarah came through the door. "Are the arrangements all right? You didn't come back, Margie, and I thought Hannah had found something wrong"

Hannah smiled briefly. "Thank you both, but do you think we'll have enough time before Saturday, since today is Tuesday and too late to get anything done? We may not be able to get the grave dug, or get a parlor at the funeral home. Also what about a preacher?"

Margie patted Hannah's shoulder. "Don't take on any more worry. I'll get on it first thing in the morning. Most funeral homes have grave digging crews that they use in family cemeteries and in the larger cemeteries they have their own, so that won't be a problem."

Hannah sat listening but it didn't seem to register. Suddenly she looked up. "I'm sorry girls but I just can't think about this right now. What you have looks fine. I'm going to bed before I make a fool of myself."

Sarah looked at Hannah. "That's the best idea you've had in a long time." She looked at her watch. "Its eight forty-five and you have slept very little since all this happened; especially since Freddie's been in jail."

Hannah smiled tiredly and looked at Margie. "Sarah's been spying on me again."

Margie got up from the sofa apologetically. "I'm sorry. I didn't mean to stay so long. Please forgive me."

Hannah rose and put an arm across Margie's shoulders. "Now Margie, we want none of your apologies. You know you like being with us as much as we like having you here. I don't know why you don't just come and stay with us."

Margie's eyes widened. "You really mean that don't you?"

"I certainly do, Margie, with all my heart."

Margie crimped her lips together. "If I had a daughter I'd want her to be just like you, Hannah."

Sarah looked at Margie and smiled. "You're never in the way out here. Why don't you spend the night? There's a spare bedroom."

Margie felt so loved, as if she really had a family. But she didn't want to abuse the privilege. "I can't spend the night or move in with you two. It is tempting, but you have enough on your hands without putting up with an old woman like me."

"Old? You're not old, Margie. You look young enough to be my sister," said Hannah as she stepped back to have a full view of Margie.

"Steve Hammer thinks you're young, too. Don't try to use that old bit as an excuse," kidded Sarah.

Margie laughed and slapped her shoulder. "You'd better not say anything about that to anyone, or you'll have to answer to a very upset friend."

Margie left with both Hannah and Sarah begging her to drive carefully. "We need you. You just don't realize how much help and comfort you have been," said Hannah, as Sarah nodded in agreement.

CHAPTER 12

AFTER MARGIE LEFT, HANNAH AND SARAH were tired and decided to go to bed early. "We've had a long day, Hannah, and also a very eventful day. Just think, this morning we hadn't made any funeral arrangements, and Margie Meadows hadn't become such a good friend."

Hannah nodded. "I guess we should have listened to the news to see who else is getting arrested, but I'm too tired. As you and I know from the preaching of Preacher Seth Adair, the Good Lord sees all things and vengeance is His, so I'm just going to try to keep it out of my mind and only worry about Freddie.

Sarah put her arm around Hannah's shoulders. "Let's just both forget that CEE ever existed. Well, no, I don't want to forget Margie Meadows, do you, Hannah?"

Hannah momentarily leaned her head against Sarah's shoulder and then straightened up as they climbed the stairs together. On the way up Hannah said, "No, Sarah I certainly don't want to forget Margie. I think she's had a really sad life."

They parted on the landing after saying good night and whatever was going on anywhere else in Beckley was closed off by sleep.

There wasn't any sleep for the Mitchell family living in the elite section of town though. When Thomas Mitchell walked out of Sabrina Draper's office he was shocked and fuming. "Those damn bumbling idiots! Asking me if I was having an affair instead of trying to find out who killed Bill Larkin," he muttered in chagrin. Thomas realized that Sabrina Draper had looked like a corpse as they wheeled her out and thought she must have used too much cocaine.

"That smartass, who calls himself a federal inspector, talking in that insulting way made me mad as hell. Besides who would have thought Sabrina Draper was stupid enough to carry cocaine around in her purse," snorted Thomas in disgust.

By the time he was in his car and driving away, he had calmed down enough to think rationally but he was still mumbling aloud.

"Somebody in the corporation is trying to cover up something big. I don't believe Sam Henson pushed the Blennoc Project onto Bill Larkin just to get rid of Sabrina Draper. I think she knows what was going on, but I sure as hell didn't get to find out."

When he arrived home he tried to act normal, but he had a weird uneasy feeling. He told his wife, Beatrice that he had already eaten when she asked if he wanted something, but he looked so uneasy that Beatrice was concerned. "What's wrong, Thomas?" asked his wife, for the third time.

"What? Oh, I'm sorry, dear. I've just been trying to puzzle something out," replied Thomas, trying to be more attentive.

Beatrice looked at him and realized he was not only troubled but tired as well. "Well, since you've already eaten let's just make it an early night. A good night's sleep cures many problems."

Thomas put his arm around Beatrice and looked at Katrina. "You have one smart woman for a mother and a good-looking one also."

The family all seemed to be more relaxed and cheerful as they gathered around the table for breakfast the next morning. Katrina looked at her father and grinned. "Mom was right, Dad. A good night's sleep really makes things look better, doesn't it?"

Missy, the youngest member of the family yawned widely. "It doesn't seem any better to me than it did last night."

Thomas looked at her and smiled. "It's much better than it was last night, but you wouldn't know because you were in bed when I got here."

"I was tired. Our game was long last night and the cheerleaders had to stay longer than usual," said Missy.

"Poor little you," said Katrina and put her arm around her sister.

They had just finished eating when the door bell rang. Their maid, Mildred, answered the door. She ushered in Sergeant McCauley and Steve Hammer.

Thomas arose from his seat as Mildred went to the door. He walked into the living room, saw the two officers, and stopped. "What now? I think I told you yesterday that I would answer no further questions without my attorney," he stated coldly.

"Things have changed, Mr. Mitchell. The chief wants you picked up as a person of interest in the poisoning of Sabrina Draper," said Sergeant McCauley.

Beatrice gasped in shock. "Who is poisoned?"

Thomas put his hand on her shoulder. "Now don't get upset, dear. This is all related to Bill Larkin's death. Sabrina Draper was Bill's assistant, and this is because I had supper with her yesterday."

"So, that's why you didn't want anything to eat." She looked at the two men at the door.

"Why are these men here? You can't be picked up for questioning just because you ate supper with someone," Beatrice said in a trembling voice.

"Mrs. Mitchell, we needed to talk to Miss Draper and your husband since they both work at Civic Enterprise Endeavors. When we met them and began questioning her she fainted, or so we thought. The Rescue Squad was called and they took her to the hospital. Your husband left and then after finding her purse we went to the hospital, taking her purse with us. The attending physician told us they found not only cocaine in her system but also poison. Since Mr. Mitchell was the last person known to be with her the chief wants him brought in for questioning," explained Sergeant McCauley.

"Thomas, did you know that woman used cocaine?" asked Beatrice.

Thomas stood mutely thinking. "Beatrice, I don't think either of us should say anything else until our attorney gets here."

"Call your attorney, Mr. Mitchell, and tell him to meet you downtown," said Steve.

Thomas gave him a malevolent stare and picked up the phone. Beatrice stood as if frozen in place, and when Thomas replaced the phone and turned, he saw that she had tears on her cheeks.

"I can't believe this, Thomas. What if that woman . . ." Beatrice stopped and turned toward Steve.

"She's not dead, is she?" she asked.

"No, Mrs. Mitchell, but nobody is allowed to see her. She's in intensive care," replied Steve.

"There's no need for Beatrice to come, is there?" asked Thomas.

"No, we don't need to question her. The chief only said to bring you in for questioning," replied Sergeant McCauley.

Katrina had not risen from the table when the doorbell rang, but now she rose quickly and entered the living room to encounter the angry look on her father's face as he put on his coat. She knew Sergeant McCauley, but not the other man who had turned with her father and gone out the door with Sergeant McCauley behind them. Seeing her mother's pale face she went to her and wrapped her in a loving embrace.

"Mom, what's going on?"

Beatrice's face was chalky, but she put her arm around Katrina and together they followed Thomas and the officers out the door. She stood on the entry steps as they pulled out of the driveway. Looking on in muted shock Beatrice tried to speak calmly.

"Katrina, your dad had dinner with Sabrina Draper last night and now she is in the hospital. She has been poisoned. That's why they are taking your father in for questioning."

"Poisoned? First Mr. Larkin's wife, then Mr. Larkin, and now his assistant have all been poisoned. They're stupid if they think dad did it, but I guess they'll question everybody with a connection. They should have arrested that Nicole Henson. She's the one that got Freddie Larkin arrested," stormed Katrina.

As mother and daughter turned to walk back into the house, Beatrice suddenly stopped and gasped in shock. "Katrina, you said Mrs. Larkin. Did somebody try to poison her? I haven't heard that."

"Nobody knows it yet," replied Katrina grimly.

"How come you know it, then?" asked Beatrice curiously.

"Mom, you are not to breathe a word of this, but I saw her folder when she was in the hospital and almost died. I think somebody had been slowly poisoning her," said Katrina.

"Poor soul, she's not had time to fully recover and now her husband is dead. Didn't the doctors report that she had been poisoned? I thought they had to," said Beatrice.

"I heard two of the doctors talking, and they said there were traces of poison found in her stomach, but some medicines have small amounts of poison. Also, by the time they had her in the hospital and had time to test everything, Mrs. Larkin had vomited most of it out of her system." The two women walked arm-in-arm back into the house.

"What will they do to dad?" asked Katrina.

Beatrice had trouble talking since the tears she was holding in seemed to be choking her. "Your uncle Jerry will meet him at City Hall. Your dad felt that he would be back shortly. I almost fainted when they said your dad had to go down town for questioning."

"Why, Dad? I mean, other than having dinner with her, he had no connection with Sabrina Draper, did he?" asked Katrina.

"She works for CEE, but I don't really know why Thomas was having dinner with her. The police were questioning everyone in the company and when they saw the two of them together, they decided to talk to both of them. When the police started to ask her some questions, the Draper woman suddenly fainted or something. They called the rescue squad and took her to the hospital," related Beatrice.

"Did dad go to the hospital?" asked Katrina.

"No, you were here when he came home last night. We all went to bed early thinking it would all be better this morning," said Beatrice.

"So, what brought them here so early this morning?" Katrina looked worried.

Beatrice still stood with her arm around Katrina's shoulders. "They said the chief of police told them to bring him in for questioning because your dad was the last person with her," said Beatrice, sighing tiredly.

Although Katrina was afraid for her father, her concern at the moment was for her mother, who couldn't keep her tears at bay. Katrina again put her arms around her.

"Don't worry, Mom. Uncle Jerry is one of the best lawyers in the state, so dad will be home soon."

"I'll have a few questions to ask him myself when he gets home," stated Beatrice. "He has never mentioned this Draper woman to me."

"Mom, surely you don't think Dad would look at another woman. You know he is crazy about you," chided Katrina.

Beatrice kept seeing the pallor of Thomas's face when Hammer was telling about him having supper with this woman. "I've never doubted your father's faithfulness, Katrina, but he acted funny when the detective said he was with this woman. I'm not going to accuse him, but I know that some men stray as they begin to reach a certain age. There's always the first time, Katrina. I certainly hope you're right, though."

Katrina hugged her mother tighter. "Mom, it was probably a business meeting. I just know Dad is not seeing another woman."

CHAPTER 13

The previous evening, Margie Meadows had driven away from Hannah's house smiling. She felt so good being with Hannah and Sarah. "It was almost like being a part of a family."

She was eager to go to work the next morning. James would be back. This gave her such a feeling of comfort and she smiled happily. She entered her office and saw that James's light was on. She hurriedly put her things away, turned on her word processor, picked up her steno pad and pencil and went straight to James' office. She hesitated for moment and then tapped on his door before she opened it.

James looked up from the letter in his hand and smiled. "Good Morning, Margie. I see you've held down the fort."

"I've tried, sir. Did you have a good trip?"

James stood up. "I did. It was a good trip and a profitable trip. We have a new business venture that wants help."

"I guess you'll want Bill . . . Margie gulped and put her hand over her mouth then quickly jumped up and ran out of the room. James Harrison saw that she was in distress.

Margie wasn't called back into the office until an hour later. The intercom blared, "Margie, bring your pad and pencil, please." Within minutes Margie Meadows, the super efficient secretary, was covering page after page with the hieroglyphic language of shorthand. There was now no evidence of tears or any other emotion. She was the epitome of efficiency and control. When James stopped talking Margie waited an imperceptible second and then closed her pad, saying, "Is that all, sir?"

James Harrison nodded and then smiled. "Work is very healing, don't you think?"

Margie smiled slowly. "It is and I thank you."

Back in her office she stayed busy until lunch time and then she arose from behind the word processor and went to the small kitchenette down the hall and put on a pot of coffee. Suddenly she remembered that she was to call her pastor and also Blue Ridge Funeral Home, but thought she should call Hannah first.

Margie returned to her desk and dialed Hannah Larkin's number. When Hannah answered Margie was relieved. She'd been feeling uneasy and didn't know why, but felt she should call Hannah. "How are you this morning, Hannah? Good. I'm just calling to see if the arrangements are still the same or have you and Sarah thought about something we may have left out."

"No, Margie, we didn't change anything. Sarah and I were tired and we didn't even listen to the news. I guess we were afraid we might hear something else to upset us," said Hannah. "We both enjoyed having you with us last night and want you to visit again soon."

"I will and thank you. I enjoyed it too, but right now I'm going to get busy. Have a good day."

Margie got out the list that she and Sarah had made on arrangements for Bill Larkin's funeral. She called the funeral director, and they arranged the service for Saturday at one o'clock if she could find a minister. Since it was already

Thursday, Margie feared there would not be enough time, but the funeral director told her there should be.

Feeling a little easier, Margie smiled and went back to her work. She was surprised when James Harrison came to her office a half-hour later.

"Margie, if anyone should want me I'm going to see Sam Henson." He stood looking at his watch for a moment as if undecided. "It's almost three o'clock. Do you think I'll be docked?"

Margie gave him a watery smile. "The way people are being poisoned, I think I'd be careful."

"I may not be back in this evening. If I don't make it back, hold down the fort."

Margie sat thinking how strange Mr. Harrison's actions and words had been. "It was almost like he wanted me to make note of the time he was leaving. Then that 'if I don't make it back,' statement, surely he didn't have some premonition or something like that."

She sat deep in thought, but her hands were unconsciously busy drawing on her desk blotter. When she looked down she had a picture of James and out from him a smiley face with 2:45 PM inside it. She sat stunned. *Why did I do that? It's as though a note should be made of the time he left,* she thought, but she didn't erase her drawing as she normally would.

Instead she rose from her desk and went to look out the window. She noted that James' car wasn't in his parking spot and thought it unusual that he would go to Sam Henson's office. "Usually Sam comes over here," she said aloud. Then she remembered that she hadn't called her pastor and turned back to her desk and picked up the phone.

Reverend Willis answered the phone. Margie had been expecting to speak to his secretary and was stunned for a moment. "Reverend, you startled me. I thought I'd be speaking to Jeanie. This is Margie Meadows."

"I sent her on an errand. Is there some way I can help you?" Margie explained the situation and asked if he could conduct Bill's funeral at one o'clock on Saturday.

Reverend Willis assured her that he was free and would gladly conduct the funeral. She thanked him and hung up. Then she called Hannah's number and again Hannah answered. "Hannah, Blue Ridge Funeral Home has the funeral scheduled for one o'clock on Saturday and Reverend Perry Willis, my pastor, will conduct the funeral. Do you think that time will be all right with Freddie?"

Hannah sighed with relief. "Yes, it will be fine and thanks so much. When this is over I may be able to relax and start living again."

When Margie hung up the phone she looked at the clock and thought, *well, its five o'clock and James isn't coming back, I guess, so I may as well go home.* She started getting her desk in order as she did every evening, but James or rather Mr. Harrison was still on her mind. *I'd better stop thinking of him as James. I might slip up sometime and that would be awful.*

She left the office smiling since she had helped Hannah and soon she was in her car. The smile disappeared as James Harrison's last words to her popped back into her mind. *They sounded ominous, even though he didn't really say anything ominous. I guess it was his behavior. He has never left early before, and it seemed as if he was stressing the time and where he was going. I don't trust Sam Henson one little bit, but he wouldn't hurt Mr. Harrison, surely*, thought Margie as she drove toward Oak Hill.

Soon she arrived at her apartment complex just off Route 16. She had just gotten in the door and put her coat and purse away when the phone rang. She looked at the caller I.D. *Jill; I guess Sam Henson must have let her come home early today. I'd better answer it*, thought Margie as she picked up the phone.

"Hello, Jill," said Margie, smiling at the phone, glad to hear her friend's voice.

"Where have you been? I've been calling you since yesterday. I was beginning to get worried," said Jill.

"I've been at work today, but if you mean yesterday, I had dinner with Hannah Larkin and her friend, Sarah Preston. I just now walked in the door," explained Margie.

"Margie, why are you getting so involved with those people? I know you have a soft heart for the underdog, but don't you think you're carrying this helping too far?"

Margie paused. "No, Jill, I don't think so. They need me and I like to feel needed. They're really nice and are so distraught over Bill Larkin."

"What are you going to do if the boy is found guilty? That will devastate you. Seems to me you're asking for whatever you get. You know I wouldn't say it if I didn't worry about you," said Jill.

"Freddie Larkin did not kill his father," blurted Margie angrily.

"See, there you are already getting upset with me, your best friend. I just want you to be careful," cautioned Jill.

Margie took a long breath. "I'm sorry, Jill. I know you want the best for me. Freddie didn't kill his father, though. The trial will prove that, but I'm sure you think I'm nuts."

"I can see I can't change your mind, so I'll just say I'm glad you're home. I know you don't like being out after dark and you were certainly out after dark last night. That's one reason I was so worried."

"Thanks, Jill. You're a good friend and I do appreciate you. Don't be mad, please. I promise to let you know the next time I break curfew," said Margie, laughing.

Jill laughed too. "Go to bed, you nut case. I'll talk to you tomorrow."

Margie spent a fitful night. She had one scary dream after another. She was thankful when the alarm went off at six-thirty the next morning.

She made breakfast and performed her usual morning routine, but stayed on edge the entire time. *What is wrong with me?* She wondered as she drank the last sip of coffee, rinsed her cup and grabbed her purse as she left the apartment.

When she arrived at the office, the building seemed quiet. She took the elevator up since she was still tired. As she approached Mr. Harrison's office and saw no lights on, she froze in amazement.

"I've never arrived for work before James in the twenty years I have worked for him. I hope he isn't sick." She inserted the key and opened her door.

She set everything ready for the day and went to James's office for the folder containing the information about the new business. At nine o'clock she finally dialed his home and waited for an answer. It rang eight or nine times with no answer. She called Thomas Mitchell's office.

When Shirley Mays, Thomas's secretary, answered, Margie asked if Thomas was in. Soon Thomas Mitchell was on the line.

"Mr. Mitchell, have you seen Mr. Harrison this morning?" she asked.

"No, I haven't. Isn't he in, yet?" Thomas asked.

"No, he isn't and it's the first time in twenty years that I've gotten to the office before him. I called his home and there's no answer either. Should I call the police?" she asked.

"Was James all right when he left yesterday afternoon?" asked Thomas.

"Yes, he was going to see Sam Henson. He left a little before three which was also unusual. Do you think I should call Mr. Henson just in case he didn't get to see him yesterday and decided to stop by his place this morning?" Margie wondered aloud.

Thomas looked at his watch and saw that it was nine-thirty. He wanted calling the police to be the last resort, and he certainly didn't want Margie to call Sam Henson.

"Margie, call Jerome Judson, James's lawyer. Maybe James went to see him. Call me after you talk to Judson."

Margie dialed Mr. Judson's number, and when his secretary had put her through to him, Margie asked, "Mr. Judson, have you talked to Mr. Harrison this morning?

"No. Why do you ask, Miss Meadows?" replied Mr. Judson in alarm.

"Mr. Harrison hasn't come in to work this morning. I called his house but there was no answer. This is just so unusual. I called Mr. Mitchell and he said to contact you," Margie said in a shaky voice.

"I think you'd better call the police, Miss Meadows. James called me at home last night and dictated a will to me. I asked him if anything was wrong and he said, 'nothing that I can't fix.' I worried about him, even though he seemed all right. Go ahead and call the police, Miss Meadows. I fear something is wrong."

Margie was so agitated that she forgot what Mr. Mitchell had said and dialed 911 before she called him. She asked for Sergeant McCauley and when he answered, Margie let out her held breath. Now she could talk to a friend.

"Keith, Mr. Harrison didn't come into work this morning. I have called his house and there is no answer. I called Mr. Mitchell and he said to call Jerome Judson, Mr. Harrison's lawyer. Mr. Judson said that James called him last night at home and dictated a will to him. Mr. Judson felt I should notify the police."

"Margie, try to stay calm. I'll go out to his house. He may have fallen or there are numerous possibilities so just keep this quiet until we know something," said Keith.

"I forgot. Mr. Mitchell told me to call him after I talked to Mr. Judson. Do you want me to call him?"

"Yes, but tell him to not say anything until I get back to you," Keith replied.

Margie called Thomas Mitchell and relayed the information she had received. She then tried to continue on with the usual work. An hour later the phone rang and Keith said quietly, "Margie, we found Mr. Harrison. He . . . he is dead. He's been shot."

Margie dropped the phone and laying her head on the desk she cried almost as hard as she had when she learned that Bill Larkin was dead. She was still crying when Thomas Mitchell came through the door.

"I see you've heard the news," said Thomas, but not seeing the television's blinking lights he thought, "Maybe she hasn't heard it yet."

Margie mumbled, "Yes, I know, James is dead." She started crying again.

"Margie, when I heard the newscast I thought I'd better come up. I know how much you cared for James. I thought it might hit you pretty hard, and I can see that it has." He replaced the receiver which Margie had left dangling, and took a seat in front of her desk.

Margie raised her head, pulled a Kleenex from the box on her desk, and blew her nose. "Mr. Mitchell, I've had this weird feeling ever since he stopped by my desk as he left yesterday." She looked down at the blotter on her desk and pointed.

"See, he strongly stressed the time as he was leaving and I, for some reason, wrote it here on this blotter and circled it. He also made sure that I knew he was going to see Sam Henson."

Thomas sat with the tips of his fingers pressed together in a steeple as his mind skittered across all the information he had gathered on Sam Henson.

"Margie, don't be surprised if you hear that Henson has been arrested," stated Thomas.

"Sam Henson! Surely he didn't do this . . . I mean he couldn't have, since James was shot," Margie stated, shivering violently.

"No, I'm not saying that Sam . . . What did you say? How do you know that James was shot? The reporter only said that he was found dead in his home," said Thomas suspiciously.

Margie looked up. "Don't look at me like that, Mr. Mitchell. Sergeant McCauley called me, but he may not want anyone else to know. Please, let's just keep it between us."

"Yes, it's best that nobody else knows how he died. I'll not say a word, and don't you become upset again and tell anyone else," cautioned Thomas. He walked to the window and looked out over the city of Beckley and thought about how often James Harrison had talked about his love for it.

"James often told me that getting to Beckley was the best thing that ever happened to him," mused Thomas.

"I know. He talked about Beckley to me, too. I think he had a miserable life until he came to Beckley," said Margie and started crying again.

"Margie, let's just go home. We'll stay closed until after the funeral. That's the respectful thing to do, don't you think?" asked Thomas.

Margie blew her nose again and nodded her head. "That makes two funerals. I just made the arrangements for Bill Larkin's funeral for Saturday, and I just don't think I can come to work until all this is over, anyway."

"Well, I'm telling you to go home. We're closed until further notice," stated Thomas adamantly.

"Thank you, Mr. Mitchell. I'm glad you are here to take over," said Margie.

The words "take over" hit Thomas like a ton of bricks. That was what he was trying to do by seeking information from Sabrina Draper. Now a load of guilt enveloped him and he turned and walked dejectedly out the door and down the stairs.

CHAPTER 14

HANNAH TOLD SARAH THAT MARGIE HAD called and the funeral was all arranged for one o'clock Saturday. Sarah's first question was, "Do you think they will let Freddie out to attend his dad's funeral?"

"I don't know, Sarah, but Keith McCauley said he would get him out if he could. I'll call him in the morning."

The two women listened to the news and heard the report that Sabrina Draper was in the hospital in intensive care. "I wonder what happened to her. Do you reckon she got so scared that she had a heart attack?" asked Sarah.

Hannah grabbed Sarah's arm. "Did you hear that? Thomas Mitchell has been taken in for questioning. He must have been friends with that woman too."

Thomas Mitchell certainly did not have friendly thoughts of Sabrina Draper when he arrived at the police station. He was glad to find Jerry Fletcher, his brother-in-law and attorney, waiting for him. Thomas introduced the police chief and the other two officers to Jerry before they were all seated.

"What's this all about?" asked Jerry, looking at Sergeant McCauley.

Sergeant McCauley started out with Bill Larkin's death and filled him in up to the time that he and Steve Hammer had gone to Thomas Mitchell's house.

"Why did you feel that Thomas should be arrested?" asked Jerry, giving the chief a narrow look.

Chief Donaldson, for some reason, wanted to sit in on this interview and now sat up straighter in his chair. "These two officers have been investigating every employee of the CEE Corporation. Inspector Hammer has done more than Sergeant McCauley, but they have both been working on the case. They knew they would need to talk to both Mr. Mitchell and Miss Draper so when they saw them together they decided to talk to them both at the same time. They went to Miss Draper's office where she and Mitchell were to meet the officers. Mitchell was the only person with the Draper woman until these officers arrived and, therefore, the only person who had a chance to do anything to her. I'm not saying that he did, but we only have his word that she already had the cocaine. He may have given it to her."

Thomas jumped to his feet, but Jerry reached out his arm to restrain him. "Sit down, Thomas. Let me handle this," said Jerry, looking stunned.

Turning back to the chief, he said, "Thomas Mitchell would never, ever have anything to do with not only cocaine but any kind of recreational drugs. I know that for a fact. You don't have fingerprints or anything substantial except Thomas was with her. You can't hold Thomas if you don't have more than that, chief, and you know it."

Jerry faced the chief, frowning. "Well, do you have any real evidence? Thomas is not going to leave town."

If Hannah and Sarah had seen the ease with which Thomas Mitchell was released they would have been outraged. Freddie was working and found his dad dead when he came home. The shock of that was bad enough, but two days later he was arrested and Thomas Mitchell only had to answer a few questions. This would have made Hannah more certain that power or clout got people out of lots of things.

Soon Jerry and Thomas were back in the car heading for the Mitchell residence. Thomas sat in a deep study. "Jerry, I don't know how to explain to Beatrice why I was having supper with Sabrina Draper."

"Why were you?" asked Jerry.

"I had suspected that something wasn't quite right about one of our businesses, and this woman had been working in that business with Sam Henson. I thought I might be able to get something out of her if she knew anything, and I was pretty sure she did."

"Is this the only time you've had supper with her?" questioned Jerry, not looking at Thomas since he was driving.

Thomas sat thinking furiously. *It is the first time I've had supper with her, so that won't be a lie.* He answered, "Yes, it is."

"Just tell Beatrice the truth. She's never had reason to doubt you before, so I'm sure you won't have a problem there," replied Jerry as he pulled into Thomas' driveway.

Thomas wished he'd never gotten involved. He could have run for the Senate without being president of CEE or any other corporation. Now, he was in a mess and if Beatrice found out that he'd taken Sabrina Draper dancing and other places, she'd never trust him again. Thomas was worried but he intended to keep that to himself.

He got out of the car and leaned in the window to grasp Jerry's hand. "Thanks, Jerry. I owe you big time."

Jerry shook his hand and grinned. "You can always increase my retainer if you feel that grateful."

Thomas smiled at his best friend and brother-in-law as he said, "In your wildest dreams, brother, in your wildest dreams." Thomas stood in the driveway until he saw the tail lights of Jerry's car recede down the street then turned wearily toward his front door.

Before he could put his key in the lock, Katrina opened the door. "Dad, thank God! We have been so worried."

Thomas hugged his daughter, saying, "I'm so sorry, precious. I'll explain what happened if you'll let me in."

They went through the glass doors of the foyer into the hall and on into the living room. Beatrice was sitting in a recliner near the fireplace. She got up as they came in. When he gathered her into his arms, she began to cry brokenly.

"Oh Thomas, I've been so shocked, angry, and defeated that I can't even think rationally," she said in a tear-choked voice.

Thomas held her close and rubbed her back in the way that had always given her comfort. "I understand, dear. It shocked me too, and made me mad. But why do you say defeated?"

Beatrice pulled away from him and went toward the sofa. Thomas followed her and sat beside her.

"Maybe that isn't the right word. I feel betrayed."

"Betrayed? Honey, surely you don't believe that I had anything to do with Larkin's death," stated Thomas in amazement.

"No, Thomas, I don't think you had anything to do with that, but I thought that you and I always talked everything out. I thought I knew as much about you as you knew about me. But I was wrong, wasn't I?" questioned Beatrice.

"No, you aren't wrong, Beatrice. I didn't have anything to tell you because I couldn't find the proof of what I suspected. I still don't have any proof. That's why I was eating with Sabrina Draper," explained Thomas.

Beatrice was just staring at him. Thomas got irritated. "Beatrice, do you tell me of every little problem you have at work? No, I'm sure you don't. We only really see each other on the weekends, most of the time, anyway. Even then we always attend church and have other activities. This was something I suspected and was trying to find out whether my suspicions had any validity."

Katrina had been sitting in a chair across from them and as yet had not spoken at all. But now she said, "I thought this Sabrina worked with Bill Larkin, but you are saying she worked with Sam Henson."

Thomas turned his head. Giving Katrina a startled look, he said, "How did you know she worked with Bill Larkin? Oh, I forgot. The paper gave that information didn't it? Well, she started working for Sam Henson, but he turned over the entire project to Bill and sent Sabrina with the project."

"Do you think Bill was doing something dishonest?" asked Katrina.

"No. I'm more inclined to think he was about to catch somebody that was doing something dishonest. I felt that the Draper woman knew about whatever it was. I was trying to find out, so I took her out to eat."

Beatrice had sat listening in rapt attention. Now she asked, "Was yesterday the only time you've had supper with her?"

Thomas felt drained and knew he was pale, but the shade lamp didn't give off a lot of light and he hoped it didn't show. "Yes, Beatrice. Yesterday was the first and only time I have taken her to supper, and I wish I hadn't done that. If I had known she used cocaine, I certainly would not have taken her anywhere. I wouldn't have had anything at all to do with her."

"What will happen now, Dad?" asked Katrina.

"Well, I suppose they will keep investigating and delving into every aspect of the corporation, and then they'll have a trial. They couldn't hold me and I heard today that Freddie Larkin is going to get out on bail. I guess we will just have to wait and see what happens."

Beatrice said, "I made some coffee while you were away, but I can make you a fresh cup if you want it."

Thomas sighed. "No thanks, sweetheart. I'm really tired. I think I'll just go to bed. Are you coming?"

"I'm waiting for Missy to call. She went to spend the night with her friend, Sandy Barbour and promised to call when she got there."

"I'll wait with you," said Thomas just as the phone rang. Katrina answered and it was Missy.

Beatrice rose when he did. Thomas took her hand as they walked out of the living room together.

Katrina still sat in deep thought. She hadn't told her parents but she had been to the jail to see Freddie Larkin. She and Freddie had gotten close since that day she had met him in the park. She had told Freddie then about what she had overheard in the lab, about poison in his mother's system. He had promised to keep it to himself, and she knew that he had. They had gone to lunch the day she met him in the park and several evenings she had gone to the jail to see him since then, but they had agreed that since their parents worked with CEE it would be best to keep their meetings secret.

Katrina had felt so bad when Freddie had been arrested. Freddie had told her about the wonderful relationship he and his father had before he met Nicole Henson.

"At first, I really did not want to meet her, but Sam Henson was Dad's boss and I did it for Dad and to be completely honest, for myself as well. Nicole is a pretty girl," explained Freddie and then dropped his head. "I wish I'd never met her though."

"I've met Nicole Henson, Freddie, and if ever there was a sneaky bitch she is one," stated Katrina angrily.

"In front of my parents she was the epitome of a well bred young lady. I bet that was her act in front of your parents, too, wasn't it?" asked Katrina.

Freddie smiled grimly. "Yes, it was, but she did tell the truth about one thing. She said all the men in CEE went out on their wives."

Katrina knew that Bill Larkin had been cheating on his wife because she had seen him with Sabrina Draper one night as she passed the Char Restaurant. They had come out and gotten into a silver El Dorado. Katrina hadn't told Freddie that she had seen them, since he was already hurt enough.

Finally she got up and turned out the light, but stood in the dark room remembering what Freddie had told her just before he was arrested. "Sammy Shrader also told me that almost every man in administrative positions with CEE had been out with Sabrina Draper, except James Harrison."

Katrina remembered what Freddie had said when she had asked, "You mean my Dad does too?"

Freddie had looked sad when he replied, "I don't know, Katrina. I'm just telling you what he said, and I believed him. My dad was going out on Mom and Sammy's dad works with every business in the corporation."

CHAPTER 15

MUCH OF WHAT HAD HAPPENED WHEN James Harrison had visited Sam Henson's office was only revealed in further investigations, but his actions that day were described in two letters and also on a recording: one letter for his lawyer and one for Steve Hammer as well as the recording.

When James Harrison had returned from his business trip he was in a good mood. A new business wanted start-up capital and James felt it was a worthwhile venture. The next day, however, he had heard about Sabrina Draper being hospitalized, and his good mood vanished. He then had become very angry and agitated. The news indicated to Mr. Harrison that Sam Henson was about to get caught. *That fool should know I keep tabs on everybody in this corporation. He doesn't know it, but I have just learned that he has connections with a drug dealer and that kind of connection takes lots of money. The Draper woman couldn't find what I needed in the Blennoc project files. That means Sam got to them first,"* thought James and had flipped the intercom button. "Margie, can you come in here, please?"

Margie came in with her pad and pencils.

"You won't need those this time. I just wanted to ask you about something."

Margie sat waiting. "Do you recall when the corporation held that stress management conference?" asked James.

"Yes sir. It was on a Friday evening, and it ran over. I was almost six o'clock getting home," replied Margie.

James sat back and rolled a pencil around in his fingers. "Do you recall who brought the bottles of Mylanta to be used as handouts?"

"Sam Henson helped a boy bring them in, sir."

"Who gave them out? Were they just left on the table for people to pick up?" asked James.

"They were set out on the table and people could pick up two bottles per person. We ran out. Later Sabrina Draper asked if there were any more. I told the errand boy to ask Sam if he had more. He came back with two bottles in a brown bag. I gave it to Sabrina," explained Margie.

"Did the boy say who he got them from?"

"I didn't ask him. I'm sorry, sir. I should have, but I just didn't think as long as I had some for her." Margie spoke in a low apologetic voice.

"Who hired the boy and who was he?"

Margie shook her head. "Mr. Harrison, I assumed that Sam hired him, since he came in with Sam carrying one of the boxes. But I can't say for certain. Anyway, Sam didn't introduce him, so I don't even know his name."

James rose from his chair and turned to look out the window for a few minutes. Then he turned back to Margie. "Well, don't worry, Margie. None of this was your fault. I just knew that you would tell me the truth if I asked you. You've been a big help. Thank you."

Margie got to her feet and quietly left the room and walked sedately down the hall to the restroom. There she pressed her hand over her mouth to keep from crying.

"He trusted me, but I didn't tell him the truth. I don't know what he will do when he finds out. I wish to God I'd never overheard that conversation," she whispered as tears ran unchecked down her cheeks.

Margie finally came out of the restroom and went back to her office. She couldn't focus on work, however. Finally she picked up the phone and dialed Raleigh General Hospital.

Margie asked to speak to the nurse in ICU. "I'm a friend of Sabrina Draper. I'm just checking to see if she is improving," stated Margie.

"What's your name, and how do you know Miss Draper?" asked the voice on the other end.

"I'm secretary to James Preston Harrison, President of CEE, her employer, and he and I are concerned about Miss Draper."

"Miss Draper is still in a coma, but her vital signs are improving. That is all I can tell you," replied the nurse or whomever she had been talking to.

"Thank you very much. That gives us some hope, anyway," Margie said and hung up. She thought about Sabrina having the nerve to go to Bill's house after all she had done to Hannah. Margie thought she deserved what she had gotten. *I just want to protect Hannah and Freddie from anything else. They've suffered enough.*

James Harrison didn't like to see Margie Meadows upset. He knew some of the things about her life, but he didn't know why Bill Larkin's death had been so devastating. Now, he had learned enough until he was fairly certain of the cause of Bill Larkin's death. He intended to get it straightened out so that Bill Larkin's son and his widow could find some peace and also to give Margie Meadows her much deserved peace.

With these thoughts on his mind, James Harrison had stopped by Margie's office and had, for some reason, made a point of noting the time as well as where he was going and then he had left his office with a determined step. He was just as determined that Sam Henson had better have a good explanation for all the things his name was tied to. *Bill Larkin is dead and now the Draper woman has been poisoned. Sam put both of them on the project. I don't think he yet knows that a federal special investigator is on the case. I'll hire a private investigator, if I need to, but Sam doesn't know that either,* Mr. Harrison had decided as he made his way to his white BMW.

Thomas Mitchell had called Harrison at six o'clock the morning after it happened and told him about Larkin's death. Then two days later Harrison had learned that the son had been arrested. At that time Thomas Mitchell didn't know the cause of death, and it was late that evening before they heard that Bill Larkin had been poisoned. When Mylanta was mentioned, the conference on stress management was the first thought that came into James's mind.

James Harrison was upset and angry and had been all day and especially after he had spoken to Margie Meadows about the conference. As he drove, he muttered aloud. "Sam Henson mentioned in a board meeting that Mylanta would be a great handout at a conference on stress and got approval from all of us. Who would have thought that he would be that devious and evil?" James pulled into the parking lot of Henson's Hardware, which also housed Sam's office.

James had closed his car door, locked it, and stood looking around. *Sam does a lot of business just for a local hardware store. It's no wonder that he has property in northern Michigan, in Florida, and here also,* he thought as he turned to the door.

As he'd gone through the store, James noticed customers shopping in every aisle and was really impressed. When he had entered Sam's office he said, "By the number of customers in there I believe the hardware business is the one to be in."

Amazed, Sam had jumped to his feet and come from behind his desk to put out his hand, smiling broadly. "Yes, sir, it is. What are you doing here? This is a first visit, I believe."

Harrison had remained standing as Sam closed the door and said, "Sit down, James, and tell me what's on your mind."

"Sam, I just heard yesterday evening that Sabrina Draper was poisoned. Did you know that?" asked James seriously.

Taking on a pasty color, Sam had said, "No, I didn't. How was she poisoned? I just heard that she fainted and was taken to the hospital," replied Sam.

"I think she is in pretty serious condition. She's in ICU. Do you know if she has any family?" James had asked.

Sam had sat as if thinking. "I believe she did have a mother living in Matewan, but I think she died. I'm not even sure about that though," he'd said, even though he knew all about Sabrina's mother and father who were both dead.

They'd gone on to discuss how much suspicious publicity the corporation was receiving because of Bill Larkin's death and how this thing with Sabrina Draper would make it worse.

Suddenly Mr. Harrison had said, "Sam, where did you get that Mylanta that you brought to the conference on stress management? I asked Margie, and she said you and some boy brought it in."

Sam had bristled. "Are you accusing me of something, James?"

'No, but I would like some answers." James had replied and had sat waiting.

"You're the president of a corporation, not the police. I don't have to answer anything, and I don't like your attitude," Sam had stated, growing red in the face.

James had looked at Sam appraisingly. "Don't get so upset. I only wanted to know who gave that boy the two extra bottles that he got for Sabrina Draper at that conference."

Sam had seemed to relax and stepped back to sit on the edge of his desk in front of James. "Do you mean that Sabrina Draper asked for extra Mylanta at that conference? I thought there was enough there for everybody. I didn't know she asked for more," said Sam.

"I asked Margie Meadows, and she said there wasn't enough and she asked the boy to go out and see if he could get two more for Miss Draper. The boy came back with two bottles in a brown paper bag, and Margie gave those to Miss Draper. Since you had brought the Mylanta to the meeting, Margie assumed that you were the one who had gotten the two extras from somewhere. Where did you get that Mylanta, Sam?" asked James.

Sam had swung his foot back and forth, shifting his weight before replying. "Are you thinking that those two bottles were the ones with poison in them and Bill Larkin ended up being the recipient?"

"All the evidence seems to point in that direction, Sam. Bill Larkin's son said his dad brought home a brown bag with two bottles of Mylanta in it. The boy put the Mylanta in the refrigerator, and Bill's wife picked it up and the lid was missing. She poured it into a glass and Bill drank it, thinking it was milk. Doesn't that make you wonder?" James had questioned.

"Well, the bottles I brought to that conference were not in paper bags, and the lids were all sealed. I don't know where the boy got the extra bottles. I just know that he didn't get them from me. " Sam had sputtered.

"You didn't say where you got those samples Sam," persisted James.

Sam had given James a keen piercing look. "Briscoll Pharmaceuticals gave them to me. Bertie Briscoll brought them over to the conference himself. I thought it was damn nice of a big operation like that, wouldn't you?" asked Sam.

When the name Briscoll was mentioned, James's expression became more placid than usual, which surprised Sam, who expected a different reaction.

James produced an appreciative smile, "Yes, it was a very thoughtful act for an organization. Who is your contact there? You must be on good terms with somebody to get that kind of service," said James calmly.

"Well, since Bertie supplies many of our businesses with their chemical supplies, I guess I know him better than anyone else over there," replied Sam smugly.

James rose from his seat. "Well, I guess the police will ferret everything out. I just hate that people in our corporation have run afoul with the law. We've had such a good name since the outset. Sometimes people get greedy and over ambitious. That's when things begin to go wrong, isn't it, Sam?"

Sam looked James in the eye and said, "That's true. Some people get too ambitious, and some people have secrets. However, secrets are sometimes disclosed just like the ambitions and like you say, the police will ferret it all out, even secrets. I know this much, if they try to pin anything on me, I know a few secrets myself that will take some people down with me."

James walked toward the door. "You are a devious man, Sam Henson. I thought that when I first met you, and I've watched you in these last twenty-five years. You don't look for the good in people do you?" James opened the door to leave.

Sam winced. "I'm just covering my back, James. It helps to be knowledgeable about everybody; it gives you bargaining leverage."

James had turned back to look at him. "I wish you'd think about this, Sam. When you deal with a stacked deck you get caught after a while. Then the 'whole house of cards' tumbles down, and you end up destroying the things you love the most."

When Sam didn't respond, James smiled grimly. "Well, good-bye, Sam. It is your future too." Harrison had walked out of Sam's office and through the store not looking to the right or the left. For some reason everyone stopped and watched his tall receding figure walking so erectly until it reached the car. Soon Harrison was gone from sight.

Sam had come to the office door and stood with the others watching and now turned and walked back to his office. *It's almost like he's leaving for good. I must have really shaken him up* he thought and became inexplicably sad. *I wonder what he meant about 'house of cards'? He couldn't possibly know about the many branches of my operations,"* thought Sam as he turned toward his desk and picked up the phone. He held it for a moment and then slowly put it back into its cradle.

CHAPTER 16

FROM THE LETTERS LEFT FOR STEVE Hammer and Jerome Judson along with the taped recording left for Steve Hammer, it was learned that James Harrison had left Sam Henson's office and driven home slowly. His dominant thought had been to determine the best way to clear everything for Margie and the Larkin family. He also thought that what he had to do wouldn't be so good for Sam Henson.

Once inside his home he went into his study and sat behind his desk thinking. He first took the disk from his recorder and opened a drawer in his desk and took out another disk and put both in an envelope. Then he drew out several sheets of paper. He wrote one letter to Margie Meadows, one to Steve Hammer, and one to Jerome Judson. Then he got up and went into his bathroom, took a shower, and put on clean pajamas.

All the while he was thinking how old and tired he felt. "I'll need to change my will." He sighed tiredly, thinking that Sam Henson was like a Chicago politician. "He never looks for good in anyone, but he makes certain he has all the dirt, or anything that he can hold over the head of everyone he knows. Well, I'll go under, but at my own hand. I'll leave him to let the police uncover all his underhanded schemes." James Harrison was so disturbed that he had been mumbling audibly

James started to the refrigerator, but then stopped. He laughed. "What's the point? Pretty soon I'll not be hungry anymore. Pa would be glad if he was here now. He'd say, 'I should have killed you all those times I tried, then you wouldn't be where you are now.' I hated Pa, and Ma wasn't strong enough to stand up to him. I know he killed her, even though the police never could find her body. Anyway, I hope the old devil knows how far I've come from the half-naked, starving urchin that social services found in that cave.

I've lived seventy-two years and I've been blessed to have it all. I really don't mind leaving it, though. Death is just the gate to that eternal world of peace that old man Wilson talked of on our many train rides together. I learned that there are worse things than being a hobo. It's worse to be born to a drunken, sadistic maniac like Pa."

James slowly shook his head. "Like old Wilson said, 'I've already served my time in Hell,' and now I'm looking forward to rest. I have no fear of death. Pa helped death lose its power over me. I often begged the Lord to please let me die."

James went into the bedroom, turned his covers back, and sat on the side of his bed. Suddenly he stood and returned to his study. There he took out pen and paper and wrote for a while, then picked up the phone and dialed Jerome Judson, his attorney. When Judson answered, James read what he had written on the paper, and when he finished Judson wanted to know why it was so urgent.

"James, you know I will change the will, but why do you want it done at this hour?" asked his lawyer.

"I've been thinking about it for several days, and I think the person named in this new will is much more deserving. I just decided to do it while it's fresh in my mind. I've written it all down on paper as well and it's in an envelope addressed to the recipient. I'll send the same to you along with a recording that I think you'll be interested in. You may even be surprised."

Judson had to be satisfied, but still asked if he felt all right, since this was a rather unusual request. James assured Judson that he was perfectly fine and was just getting ready for bed.

"Well, if you're sure - and you sound like you are - I'll say goodnight, James. Sweet dreams, my friend.

James smiled. "Peaceful is all I ask."

He hung up the phone, opened the letter addressed to Margie Meadows and inserted the sheet of paper. He sealed and patted it, then laid it beside the one addressed to Steve Hammer. One recording he put in an envelope addressed to Steve Hammer as well and the other he put in with the letter and will addressed to Jerome Judson He sat still for a moment and suddenly laughed aloud.

"Sam Henson didn't know I often record meetings. Nobody knows that I'm hard of hearing."

Then he went straight back to his bedroom and sat down on the bed. He pulled his forty-five automatic from the table beside his bed. He sat holding the weapon he had dreamed about during those years when his father beat and kicked him so unmercifully. He had kept the gun cleaned and polished and at times was thankful that he hadn't had it when his father was alive.

"I would have been in prison for murder. I was too little to fight him. A seven-year-old boy doesn't have much chance with a grown man."

The phone rang and James looked at the caller I.D. When he saw the name, he smiled grimly. "Sorry, old friend or whatever you were, but I've finally found you out. I should have realized what was happening, but I was too trusting." He lifted the receiver and dropped it back into its cradle.

Sitting very straight, he put the barrel of the gun into his mouth, pointed it up toward his brain, and pulled the trigger. People in the building or along the street would have thought a car backfired if they heard anything at all.

The letters James had written were propped up on his desk. When Keith McCauley broke through the door he went to the study first. He saw the three letters but didn't bother with them then, but went through the other rooms until he came to the bedroom, where he stopped in stunned amazement. He went in and found James Harrison lying on his back across the bed. Keith went around the foot of the bed to the other side where James Harrison's head lay. When he moved the head, much of the back of the skull splattered the bed. Bile rose into Keith's mouth. Never having seen anything like this before, he barely made it to the bathroom and lost his breakfast. Finally the nausea eased, and he made it back into the bedroom and picked up the phone.

"He must have had this all planned. I wonder what brought him to this?" murmured Keith as he called the chief.

Keith remembered the letters he had seen. He went back to the study and picked them up. He studied them intently and wished he could open the one addressed to Steve, but he didn't.

Soon the wail of the siren, announcing the arrival of the ambulance, was loud in the street. People spilled out of their houses to gawk and find out what was going on.

Reporters from the television station and the Beckley Herald were soon there with cameras flashing. Not wanting her to find out from the TV, Keith sneaked away to the bathroom and dialed Margie.

He had already picked up the gun using his handkerchief and stowed it in a plastic bag that he found in the kitchen. He put this package away in a bedside table until he could gather other evidence from the scene.

Until he had a "go-ahead" from the chief, Keith could only tell the reporters that he had gotten a 911 call that Mr. Harrison hadn't shown up for work and his secretary was concerned.

"I can't tell you the cause of death until the autopsy has been done, but as soon as I can report anything I'll give you all a call," he promised.

An EMT said to Keith, "I guess you found him?"

"Yes. Until I moved his head he looked so neat. It looked as if he had showered and changed into his pajamas, turned his covers down, then lay back across the bed and fell asleep. He must have fallen straight back across the bed. It didn't damage his face at all, but blew the whole back of his head off."

The EMT shook his head sadly. "I don't know how somebody could do that." He shivered, looking almost as white as his assistant, as he came back from the bathroom. By this time the body was rolled into a blanket, placed on the gurney, and was being rolled out of the room. Just outside the door they stopped and one turned and looked back at the bed.

"I guess we should collect all that on the bed. I'll do it, but I'll probably puke my guts out before I finish," he said as he pulled a mask and gloves from a packet beneath the gurney and turned back into the room.

Keith was inspecting the house to make sure that nothing else was disturbed or out of place. He couldn't help hearing the gagging that was going on in the bedroom.

By this time Steve Hammer had arrived. "I got here as quick as I could. I was out near Summersville. Someone reported a car theft ring and I was investigating it."

Keith looked at him. "I'd rather have been with you. I've been sick as a dog, but Margie called me and I had to come. I didn't mind coming, but I sure didn't like what I found." Suddenly remembering the letters, he pulled them from his coat pocket.

"He left this letter for you, but I think it's more than a letter."

Steve took the letters and broke the seal on the one addressed to him. When he had finished reading it he whistled, "I sure wouldn't have expected that. In fact that's the last person I would have suspected. This town will get the surprise of their lives, since the chief has been trying to pin Bill Larkin's death on Freddie. To the chief, it is always easier to pin things on some non-entity, somebody who couldn't muck up his business deals in this town."

Then Steve pulled two small cassette tapes from the envelope. "If these reveal more than the letter our investigation is over." Keith nodded in agreement.

Both men stood thinking about James Harrison. They knew that he was well-respected and known for his charitable contributions to help children. His name was often in the paper, but very few people knew him since his picture was never in the paper. Steve walked behind Keith as they made for the door.

"Oh well, I guess it's like the Bible says, 'The great and the small are there' and death levels us all out," Steve said pensively.

Keith smiled. "I didn't know you read the Bible, Steve. I guess there are lots of things about you that I don't know, like you and Margie Meadows. Now, that was a surprise."

CHAPTER 17

WHEN THEY LEFT JAMES HARRISON'S HOUSE both McCauley and Hammer were very upset. Keith knew how much James Harrison had done for Beckley and to see him end his life in such a way made Keith very depressed. Steve was saddened as well, but having worked all over the country on special cases, was more hardened to the depths of anguish that human beings encounter.

"With what Harrison reveals in this letter, Beckley is going to have a lot of sleepless residents," said Steve.

"It makes me so angry that the chief insisted on Freddie Larkin being arrested when he knew what a shape Mrs. Larkin was in. I practically begged him to give me a few days before taking that action." Keith almost snarled with disgust.

"Our chief wanted a little-known person to pay for what some more important person was doing, or had done."

"Well, your Hannah doesn't know what we know or it would be worse for her than it is now. Are you going to try to get Freddie released for his dad's funeral?" Steve looked at Keith and saw the determined pursing of his lips.

"You bet your life I am. The chief has done everything in his power to delay Freddie's bail bond hearing, but I'm going to tackle him about releasing Freddie in my custody to attend the funeral."

Steve smiled. "That should give you some 'brownie points' with the little lady."

Keith raised his eyebrows and gave Steve a sideways grin. "I think I'm going to need more than brownie points in that area."

"Let's head straight to Chief Donaldson's office. I'm anxious to see his face when he reads James Harrison's letter to me, aren't you?" Steve looked at Keith with a narrow-eyed gleam.

"I wouldn't miss it for the world. I don't know if I should have taken Margie's letter to her first or if I should take it to the chief," said Keith as they got out of the car at the police station.

"He'll have to give Margie's letter to her, since it's addressed to her. My letter tells us almost everything we need to know anyway," answered Steve Hammer.

They entered the building, made their way to the chief's office and knocked on the door. The chief looked up and yelled, "Come in." They opened the door and walked in.

They took seats in the two chairs in front of Chief Donaldson's desk and waited for him to finish a phone call. He quickly hung up and turned glaring eyes at the two officers.

"You reported that Harrison was dead, but why were you there?" asked Donaldson looking at Keith.

"Margie Meadows, his secretary, called because Mr. Harrison didn't come in to work, and she couldn't get an answer at his home. She called Mr. Harrison's lawyer and was told to call 911."

Keith went on to tell the chief all he knew. Then Steve produced his letter. He also reported what Margie Meadows had told them about Harrison calling his lawyer, Jerome Judson, the evening before and changing his will.

Chief Donaldson picked up the letter Steve had put on his desk and began to read. Keith could have sworn that his eyes bulged as his body appeared to sag downward and his face turned deathly white. He jerked himself straight and finished reading, while breathing heavily, like someone trying to free himself from a straight jacket. When he got to the bottom, he drew an agitated breath.

"I'll be damned. Who would have thought James Harrison would have done something like this. He says he has proof of all this with his lawyer." Chief Donaldson drew a long breath and then sat staring into space.

"I think I'd better talk to the prosecuting attorney about this," he said as he arose from the desk.

"I'd like to have my copy of that letter, Chief," said Steve and when the chief looked at him with a frown, he continued. "I may need some of that information. It will save some steps in the investigation."

Chief Donaldson turned to the copy machine against the wall and opening the cover slammed the letter down. He didn't turn until he had made copies of the three pages. Turning, he thrust the originals at Steve and stalked toward the door.

"Harrison says he left proof with his lawyer. You'd better check on that first." He snarled as he went out the door, slamming it behind him.

Keith and Steve looked at each other in amazement. "Now why wouldn't he want us to have a copy? We could get it from Jerome Judson, but this will save us some time," said Keith, still puzzled. They sat down to wait and went over the contents of the letter again.

Chief Donaldson came stalking through the door in a short while and didn't even sit down. "Well, I guess that's settled. The Grand Jury is meeting and Kyle Swan, the prosecuting attorney, is going to ask for a sealed indictment. He also got the judge to issue a bench warrant. That means you can go on and make some arrests. You can pick up one person for murder and one for aiding and abetting. This is going to rock this town from one end to the other."

He turned to look out the window. When he turned back, he started moving things around on his desk. Suddenly he seemed to realize that Keith and Steve were still there and looked at them. "Well, what are you waiting for? Go on about your business," he ordered.

Steve and Keith started out to the car, but Keith turned back to the chief's office. Once there, he put his hand in his pocket and pulled out the letter addressed to Margie Meadows. He pushed the door open, stuck his head through, and was startled when Donaldson wheeled around from a file cabinet he had open and snapped, "What do you want now? I told you to go on."

"This letter was beside the one written to Steve, but since it is addressed to Margie Meadows, I thought you'd want me to take it on to her. It probably has something to do with the corporation."

Chief Donaldson thought for a minute. "Take it on to her, but tell her to keep it a secret until we need it, if we do. There may be something in it that is pertinent to the case."

Keith put the letter back into his shirt pocket and left the office. Arriving at the car, he told Steve about the chief's strange behavior, and they got into the car discussing his reaction to the entire event.

Soon they were on their way to Margie Meadows's house in Oak Hill.

"I guess you know which apartment is hers, don't you?" asked Keith, looking mischievously at Steve.

"I sure do. I don't let the grass grow under my feet when I like somebody. I'm not like you. You can barely contain yourself when you are around Hannah Larkin, but you try to hide it," said Steve.

Keith shook his head. "I don't come on to her, and you know it. The woman has just lost her husband. I'd be awfully crass and cold-hearted to mention anything now. Besides, she'll not want any part of a big rough lout like me."

By this time they were at the Glade Springs Village apartment complex. Steve directed Keith to the upper end where they parked. With Steve in the lead, they were soon knocking on door 123. Keith pulled the letter out of his pocket while they waited. Margie cracked the door and peeked out. When she saw Keith and Steve she undid the chain and invited them in.

Keith handed Margie the letter. She took it with trembling fingers and gasped as she recognized the handwriting. "Where did you find this? When did he write it?"

Keith told her about finding three letters on the desk in Mr. Harrison's study. "He must have written them last night. They were propped up against a set of law books and turned so that they would not be missed."

Tears were running down Margie's face as she reached for her letter opener. She slit the envelope open and found two letters. She unfolded the first, a long sheet of legal paper, and began to read. Suddenly, she dropped the letter and became convulsed with sobs.

Steve reached down and picked the letter up without trying to discover its contents and then sat down beside of Margie. He sat holding the letter, without reading it, until she had calmed down. Then he handed it back to her.

Margie looked up with red-rimmed eyes and said, "This is his will. It says he has left almost everything he has to me." She was almost in shock and was having trouble breathing.

Steve put his hand on her shoulder. "Can I get you a drink, Miss Meadows? You need something to help you calm down."

Margie turned and looked at him and then suddenly fell against his chest and was folded in his arms. She kept sobbing and babbling about not having any idea that James cared about her. She was getting almost hysterical and Steve looked up at Keith in silent appeal.

"Margie, do you have any nerve pills? You need something to calm you down. You're going to be sick," cautioned Keith.

Gulping and gasping for breath, Margie finally got out that she had some in her purse. Keith started looking around the room until she managed to get out the word, "Bedroom." Soon Keith was back with her purse. She tried to get it open, but dropped it. Things went flying in all directions. Seeing a pill bottle, Keith picked it up and looked at it.

"Ativan! That's a nerve pill." Margie nodded, and he went to the kitchen and got a glass of water.

"Open your mouth," he said when he returned, and like a baby bird she obeyed. Margie was still crying and trembling all over.

"I think you should go to bed and let that pill do its work. Let me help you to bed," Steve said, and Margie shook her head.

She finally drew a long breath and said, "Please call my friend Jill Dawson. Her number is in the book by the telephone"

Keith called, and when the phone was answered he said, "I'm calling for Margie Meadows. She isn't feeling well. This is Sergeant Keith McCauley of the Beckley Police." When Jill said she'd be right over, Keith hung up the phone.

Jill arrived and Keith let her in. She stood staring at Margie Meadows held in the arms of a man.

"What's happened? What's wrong with her? Who are you?" she asked, looking at Steve.

"I'm Inspector Steve Hammer. Will you see if you can get her to lie down for a while? She's taken one of her nerve pills, but she has had quite a shock."

When Jill came toward her, Steve reluctantly arose and said, "Sit here. She needs someone close to her until she calms down."

"What has happened? I mean what brought this on?" asked Jill as she took Steve's place and put her arm around Margie.

Margie raised her head and said, "Jill, my James is dead," and then slid toward the floor. Steve caught her and gently laid her on the sofa.

Jill ran to the bathroom and came back with a wet washcloth and washed Margie's face. Margie opened her eyes and looked up at Jill with an almost vacant stare. "Mommy, what are you doing here? How did you get away?"

Steve looked at Keith with a startled expression and Jill gaped in astonishment. "She's out of her head," she gasped and Keith quickly picked up the phone and dialed 911.

CHAPTER 18

WHEN THE AM BUIANCE ARRIVED, MARGIE WAS loaded into it. Jill followed the two policemen to the hospital.

Margie was soon examined, sedated, and put in a private room. Steve, Keith, and Jill sat with her. Jill looked at the two men and said, "I'm staying with Margie tonight. I'm afraid she will wake in the night and need someone."

Just then the doctor came in. "I know all of you are anxious to know what's wrong with your friend. There's nothing physically wrong. She's had a profound emotional shock, though. I think she will be all right in a short time," explained the doctor. He picked up his papers and nodded to Keith as he walked to the door.

There he stopped. "I know her friend insists on staying the night with Miss Meadows, so you two gentlemen can go on about your business. I feel sure she will be much better tomorrow," promised the doctor as he stood waiting at the door. When Keith and Steve followed him, he finally went on out the door and closed it behind him.

"Who did you say had died? Was it her husband?" asked the baffled doctor.

"You haven't seen the news, I guess," said Steve.

The doctor said that he hadn't been near a television all day. Steve then explained, "Her boss for twenty years, James P. Harrison, just died. He left a letter for her and a will, but we don't really know what was in either of them. When she read the will, she started crying and just kept getting worse. She fainted and Jill, her friend, washed her face with a cold cloth. She came around but was irrational, so we called 911."

Keith and Steve left the hospital and headed for Sam Henson's office. When they arrived the entire building was closed.

"I guess that means we go to his house, doesn't it?" asked Steve.

"I hate to arrest somebody at their home, don't you? I'll never forget having to arrest Freddie Larkin. That almost killed his mother. Still, his finger prints were all over that glass and the chief wanted him arrested," said Keith.

They talked about the arrests they had made over the years until they pulled into Sam Henson's driveway at seven o'clock. When they rang the bell a small dark woman answered the door.

"Is Mr. Henson in?" asked Steve.

"Yes, but he and the missus are having dinner. They don't like to be disturbed," the woman replied.

"We're sorry for the inconvenience, but I'm afraid we must insist," stated Steve. The woman hesitated, then stepped back and allowed them in. She then scurried away, to return soon followed closely by Sam Henson.

"You're here again, I see. I told you all I knew the last time you were here," said Sam with a martial gleam in his eyes.

"Sam, have you listened to the news this evening?" asked Keith.

Sam looked puzzled. "No. I've been away most of the evening."

"Then you don't know that James Harrison is dead?" asked Steve warily.

"James is dead? When did he die? I saw him yesterday evening and he was very much alive. What happened?" questioned Sam, turning pale.

"We found him dead in his home about ten o'clock this morning," stated Steve, watching Sam turn almost green.

"Because of some information he left, we have come to arrest you as a person of interest," said Steve.

"Arrest me? I didn't kill him. What kind of evidence? I don't care what he said," sputtered Sam, now red in the face.

"We have to remind you that what you say can and will be used against you in a court of law, so you have a right to remain silent," explained Steve.

Just then Martha came on the scene. "What is this? Sam, don't get angry. Remember your blood pressure," she chided as she turned an angry glare on Steve and Keith.

"James Harrison is dead and they are arresting me!" stormed Sam.

Martha gasped. "James Harrison! Oh my God! When did he die? We've been in Summersville almost all day. Why are you arresting Sam?"

Steve explained the circumstances of James Harrison's death, but did not reveal the cause. "He left a letter, Mrs. Henson that implicates Sam in some questionable financial dealings on the Blennoc Project."

"That damn bastard is trying to ruin me. Well, I can fix him," Sam stopped. He suddenly realized that James Harrison was dead, and nothing he said would make any difference to him. Everyone was looking at Sam as he dropped his head.

"I guess you'll come peacefully, won't you, Sam?" asked Keith and Sam raised his head and looked at Martha.

"Martha, I'll have to go, but this is just a set-up. At least they're not accusing me of killing him," stated Sam with his eyes glued to Martha's face.

Martha stood still as if in shock, and Sam stepped toward her. "Martha, listen to me. I'm innocent, so you call Ken Martin and tell him to get down to city hall." Martha nodded and began to cry. The small dark woman came and put her arm around Martha.

Sam looked at Keith and said, "Let's go then. I don't want the neighbors bugging Martha."

Sam got in beside Keith, and Steve rode in the back as they pulled away. They soon arrived at the station, and Chief Donaldson came out of his office just as they walked through the door.

As soon as Sam saw the chief he said, "Harry, tell these damn fools that I'm innocent."

Chief Donaldson grimaced. "I'm sorry. I can't do that, Sam. James Harrison left too much evidence."

Sam blanched. "What evidence? I don't know what you're talking about. I'm not saying another word until my lawyer gets here."

They all sat down to wait, but Henson was so edgy that he just couldn't keep quiet.

"If he said that I poisoned Bill Larkin he lied. I had nothing to do with that. I guess he just tried to ruin me because he didn't want me to tell about his . . ." Sam stopped when his attorney, Ken Martin, came hurriedly through the door.

The lawyer greeted everyone and sat down beside Sam. "What have you been told, and what have you said?" he asked.

Chief Donaldson stood up. "James Harrison is dead, but he left a letter with a very convincing story. He advised that we pick up Sam Henson for questioning. It seems he had Sam under surveillance. His revelations are convincing enough for the judge to issue a bench warrant. It seems that Sam has been 'cooking the books' on the Blennoc Project."

Keith interrupted. "Harrison said that Sam knows a lot about poison as well and I find that very interesting."

Chief Donaldson glared. "Don't complicate this, Sergeant McCauley. You can't arrest someone just for knowing about things."

"Hell, it's all a bunch of trumped up charges. That project was fine when I turned it over to Bill Larkin. James Harrison just wanted to get back at me because I know . . ." Sam stopped, interrupted by a warning look from Ken Martin.

Mr. Martin turned to the chief. "I guess you'll book him, but how soon can I post bail for him? I'll try to get you out on bail, Sam, but you may have to stay one or two days."

"The Grand Jury is in session and I don't know whether he can get out on bail or not," stated Chief Donaldson. He nodded to Keith and Steve. They took Sam out to the desk where all the paper work was done and Sam was assigned to a cell.

The chief remained in his office talking to Ken Martin. They appeared to be arguing as Keith walked back toward the office. He stepped to the side of the wall where he could look in but not be seen. As he watched, the chief jabbed the air with his finger, right in front of Martin's face. Keith gazed in amazement when the lawyer jumped up and reached across the desk to clutch Chief Donaldson's tie. Keith quickly opened the door to stop dead at what he heard.

"You try to pen all this on Sam and your ass will end up in jail right along with him," Martin yelled as the chief turned redder in the face.

"What's going on here? Turn him loose, Mr. Martin," ordered Keith.

Both men were red and glaring, but at Keith's order they began trying to regain control.

The chief tried to smile. "Ken thinks I should do more for Sam than I can. Just ignore our little contretemps. It's just a disagreement between friends, isn't it, Ken?" stated the chief, giving Martin a gimlet stare.

Seeing that Keith wasn't satisfied, Donaldson pushed at Martin's hold on his tie and Martin abruptly released his hold and stepped away. The chief tried to grin. "Ken thinks I have more power in this county than I do. I can't sway Judge Wilson and neither can anyone else that I know." He was free from Ken Martin, but still his face was a mottled red.

Martin seemed to relax, but gave the chief a malevolent stare. "Sure, Harry and I will settle this privately. Harry knows I mean what I say, don't you, Harry?"

Donaldson glared back, but said, "Yeah, I hear you Ken." His face was twisted into a grotesque snarl and Keith almost blanched at the evilness portrayed.

CHAPTER 19

Steve and Keith went back to their car in a very puzzled mood. They were off duty and decided to tell Hannah Larkin about Margie Meadows.

"It's almost nine o'clock. Do you think it's too late to go out there?" asked Steve.

Remembering what Freddie had told him about watching The Tonight Show every night, Keith said, "Nope. They'll be up. Besides you know they'll want to know about Margie Meadows. They have become close since Bill Larkin died. It seems like they're almost family. Don't you think that is unusual? When we stopped by there the other night I felt like I was visiting with a mother, daughter, and friend, didn't you?" asked Keith.

Steve replied absentmindedly. "Yeah, I guess so, but I'm more puzzled by what happened in the chief's office a few minutes ago. It made me think that the chief is embroiled in some of Sam's shenanigans. What do you think, Keith?"

Keith grimaced. "I don't know what to think. It's certainly more than they said. Ken Martin knows that Donaldson can't influence Judge Wilson. Nobody can influence him. I swear I've never dealt with a case that has so many angles. Right when you think you have compelling evidence against one person, someone else acts so strangely, that you're all at sea again."

"Do you think Sam Henson set Bill Larkin up?" Steve asked.

"I don't know, but James Harrison was pretty sure he did, and now seeing the chief and Martin act so suspiciously, I think there is something. I certainly don't believe the story the chief concocted, do you?"

"No, I don't, and Martin was sure hot under the color about something," replied Steve.

By this time they were pulling up into Hannah Larkin's driveway. "I hope we're doing the right thing by telling Hannah about Margie Meadows," said Keith as they got out of the car.

"So, its Hannah now, is it?" asked Steve, grinning broadly.

Keith's ruddy complexion turned even redder. "I meant Mrs. Larkin. I just misspoke it," he stammered.

Steve shadow punched him as they stepped upon the porch. "If you say so, good buddy."

Sarah answered their knock. "We're not having fish tonight, but you're welcome to left-over homemade spaghetti," she said as she ushered them into the house.

Hannah came through from the bedroom and stopped abruptly and looked at Keith. "What's happened? I know there's something wrong or you wouldn't be here."

"There was nothing wrong the other night, when we visited with all of you, Mrs. Larkin," said Keith calmly.

Hannah seemed to relax as she remembered that night. "Well, come on in and sit down. We've had dinner but we can fix you both a plate of spaghetti if you like."

Steve looked at Keith, then back at Hannah. "We didn't come here to arrest anybody, if that's what you thought. But we did want to tell you something."

Hannah took a seat on the sofa and now sat forward, tensely waiting.

"Have you listened to the television or radio today?" asked Keith. At their negative nods, Keith continued, "James Harrison was found dead in his home this morning."

"Dead? Who tried to poison him?" blurted Sarah.

"He wasn't poisoned, Sarah. He left a letter for Margie. We gave it to her and there turned out to be two letters inside the envelope. One was a will, and when she read it, she started crying. We couldn't get her to stop and she fainted. We had to call an ambulance. She is in Raleigh General Hospital right now."

Hannah jumped up from the sofa. "Sarah, we need to go to her. I'll get my purse and car keys."

"Mrs. Larkin, you can't see her right now. The doctor sedated her, and she can't have any company until tomorrow. He said it was the shock from Mr. Harrison's death and whatever was in the letter that caused the trauma."

Hannah sat down again but still looked tense. "Are you sure she's going to be all right?"

"That's what the doctor said, and her friend Jill Dawson is staying with her tonight. Should she wake during the night she'll have someone she knows with her," said Steve.

Everyone seemed to relax until Sarah asked, "How did Mr. Harrison die if he wasn't poisoned?"

Steve had stood up and now turned to look at Sarah. "He died from a gunshot wound."

"Do you know who did it?"

"We think we do, but it has not been officially proclaimed, so we can't say anything about it," explained Steve.

Steve asked if he could have a glass of water, and Hannah went to the kitchen. When she left, Steve turned to Sarah. "Didn't Freddie date Sam Henson's daughter for a while?"

Sarah turned suspicious eyes to Steve. "Yes, he did. Why do you ask?"

"I just wanted to know what Freddie thought of Sam. Did he see him very often?" asked Steve seriously.

Sarah ran her hand through her hair and rubbed her chin. "Has this anything to do with Bill's murder?"

Steve turned as Hannah came back in. "Here is the water you wanted." Hannah turned to Keith. "Do you want anything, Sergeant McCauley?"

Keith smiled at Hannah and shook his head no. He looked at Steve before turning to Sarah. "I can't tell you what, but some other evidence has come to light that casts suspicions on Sam Henson."

Sarah sat looking off into space. "I'm not really surprised from the things Freddie told us that Nicole said about him. She didn't paint a very pleasant picture of her father," said Sarah.

"You'll read it in the news tomorrow anyway, so we may as well tell you two that Henson has been arrested," Steve said.

"Do you think Henson murdered Bill?" asked Hannah.

"No, Mrs. Larkin. Henson was arrested on other charges having to do with the Blennoc Project," explained Keith. "So, if either of you mention his arrest to anyone, just say you heard it on the news."

Both Hannah and Sarah assured him that they would not say anything. So, Steve and Keith rose to leave, telling Hannah and Sarah they would keep in touch.

Hannah quickly rose from her seat and grabbed Keith's coat sleeve. "Can't you get Freddie released for his dad's funeral on Saturday? It isn't fair; not being allowed to attend his father's funeral."

Keith put his hand over Hannah's, which was still clutching his coat sleeve. "I've already put in that request and should know by tomorrow." Hannah pulled at her hand and Keith dropped his hand to his side.

"As soon as I know, I'll call, okay?" Hannah nodded and stepped back from him.

When the car pulled away, Hannah and Sarah looked at each other in amazement. "Hannah, I think Bill must have found some wrongdoing or was about to find something involving CEE, don't you?" asked Sarah.

"I don't know, Sarah, but those arrested, with the exception of Freddie, those who are now dead, and those in the hospital, were all working with CEE. That does look suspicious."

They both got up and went to the kitchen, since the dinner dishes had all been left on the table. While they washed the dishes and wiped the counter tops, Sarah suddenly stopped with a dishcloth in her hand. "Hannah, do you know if Bill brought any papers home with him? Do you remember if he had a briefcase with him the evening he died or not? I've not seen one if he did," said Sarah who had helped clean every nook and cranny of the entire house.

Every time Bill's name was mentioned, the image of him lying huddled in the floor flashed into Hannah's mind. She wheeled around and hurriedly left the room.

Sarah threw her dishcloth on the sink and ran after her. "I'm sorry, Hannah. I forgot. I didn't mean to get you upset."

Hannah turned a pale face to Sarah. "I'm all right, Sarah. I just keep seeing him there in the floor." She shook her head as if to chase away the memory.

They both sat down in the living room, their thoughts chaotic, and Sarah let out a long sigh and leaned back on the sofa. She reared up again and moved the throw pillows, but was still uncomfortable. She wriggled and scrunched until one of the sofa cushions slid sideways. She got to her feet to scoot the cushion back in place but lost her footing and fell, tilting the cushion onto the floor.

"Sarah, what are you doing? You're going to ruin my sofa," Hannah laughingly scolded. Sarah got back onto her feet to put the cushion back in place. When she picked it up, she suddenly stopped.

"Hannah, look what I found!" she exclaimed as she bent over the sofa. From where the cushion should have been she brought out a slender folder with a rubber band around it.

"Open it, Sarah. That may be what is needed to clear Freddie," ordered Hannah in a hopeful voice.

CHAPTER 20

SARAH PUT THE FOLDER ON THE coffee table. Moving the center piece around, she slipped off the rubber band and opened the folder. Hannah came and sat down beside her. Sarah read slowly, frowning in a puzzled manner.

"What does it say, Sarah?"

Sarah looked up. "It lists chemicals, plate glass, film, and frames. But since I have no idea what it is talking about, I can't see what could be wrong." Sarah kept turning the pages. She suddenly stopped.

"Here's a new name - a Bertram Briscoll, who seems to be heavily involved. His signature is on all these last pages. Did you ever hear Bill mention him?"

Hannah shook her head. "No, but Bill hadn't been talking to me about his work for a long time, especially after he took on that Blennoc Project."

Sarah put all the papers back in the folder. "I think we should put this in a safe place until we can get it to Keith and Steve, don't you?"

Hannah said she would put it in her lingerie drawer. "Nobody would think Bill would put something like that in my dresser drawer anyway."

About thirty minutes later they decided to call it a night, but still went back to make sure the kitchen was in its usual pristine order. When they were finished they decided to watch the news before retiring. They went back into the living room and turned on the TV. The newscaster came on with the information that James Preston Harrison was found dead from a self-inflicted gunshot wound.

Hannah gasped. "He shot himself? How awfully sad! The Bible says to take a life is a sin." She sat quietly listening to the report.

"Bill talked like there was nobody on earth like James Harrison. He was always talking about how much he donated to orphanages, hospitals, and all kinds of educational things for children. Bill said he was very wealthy, also. He wouldn't have been doing something dishonest, I don't think. Do you?"

Sarah doubted it, but still couldn't understand why he would kill himself. "Maybe he found out he had cancer or something like that."

As they continued to watch the news Sarah said, "Hannah, the only member we know on the CEE board who hasn't been charged with something or isn't dead or in the hospital is Thomas Mitchell."

"I thought Margie said he had been questioned and released because he was with that Draper woman when she fainted," said Hannah.

"Yeah, that's right. They didn't really arrest him, but they asked him if he would he be willing to go down to the station. He and his lawyer went. They didn't have enough evidence to arrest him like they did Freddie," said Sarah.

"Keith . . . uh, I mean Sergeant McCauley said if they hadn't found Freddie's fingerprints all over that glass that they couldn't have held him. Now he'll have to be tried, won't he?" said Hannah worriedly.

They both knew that Margie had gotten a highly recommended lawyer for Freddie and felt that he would be cleared. Still, it bothered them both.

They sat for a while puzzling and discussing this news, before deciding they would go to see Margie the next day.

That night, Hannah tossed and turned trying to get the case off her mind. Finally, she went to the dresser drawer and pulled out the folder again. She went over the report page by page and slowly began to see a pattern. Everything seemed routine except on every third month. She looked at the orders for that month and then looked at the delivery for the same month. "The order was short by three cases, yet this Briscoll signed as if it was all there," Hannah said to herself. By the time she had finished the folder, she realized why Bill had brought it home.

"It would be easy to fix this if someone checked the files, so I guess Bill wanted to have the originals," thought Hannah as she redid the folder and sat holding it. For some reason she felt it should be hidden a little better. She grinned mischievously and felt easier as she closed the drawer and returned to bed.

She finally fell into a fitful sleep in which Sabrina Draper and Sam Henson flitted in and out of her dreams. She was so tired that she overslept and Sarah, getting concerned, eventually woke her.

"You never sleep late, Hannah. I'm sorry I woke you, but I feared that something was wrong."

"It's all right. I had bad dreams all night anyway. Sarah, I looked at that folder again last night, and I found that somebody was short changing Bill on the orders every three months. Briscoll's name is signed to all the short orders," stated Hannah.

Sarah was astonished. "No wonder you didn't sleep. You may have found the reason someone wanted Bill out of the way."

Sarah had fixed bacon, eggs, and toast. "Come on, let's eat. We can't do anything with the information, but Keith and Steve can. We'll probably see them when we go to see Margie."

Hannah smiled. "Margie was so embarrassed when Steve said he'd been trying to get to know her."

"Hannah, don't you think it's strange how you immediately accepted Margie Meadows into your life?" asked Sarah.

Hannah thought about it. "Yes it is, Sarah, but honestly, I loved her the first time I really met her. I mean, Bill introduced me to her when I was pregnant with Freddie, but I just thought she was a nice lady and forgot about her. Bill would occasionally mention her name, and I would ask about her. He always talked as if she was a special kind of woman. When I was in the hospital, she sent flowers or cards almost every day. At first, I didn't know who sent them, but before I came home that sweet little nurse with the pretty voice told me they all came from Margie Meadows."

Sarah smiled. "Do you know who that nurse is, Hannah?" she asked.

Hannah shrugged her shoulders. "I know her name is Katrina, but I don't know anything else. I guess I was too sick to ask, but she sure was a sweet, pretty little thing."

"Her name is Katrina Mitchell. She is Thomas Mitchell's daughter." Sarah smiled smugly since Freddie had told her who the girl was.

Hannah looked amazed. "Well, isn't that something. It seems like every direction we look CEE has some kind of connection, doesn't it?" Hannah yawned sleepily and rose to her feet just as the phone rang and Sarah answered it.

"Hello, the Larkin residence. This is Sarah Preston speaking."

"Yes, she's here, but I'm her friend and I am trying to take care of all this if I can. Our friend, Margie Meadows, is helping us. Did she call you?" asked Sarah. "That sounds great. Yes, one o'clock on Saturday will be just fine. Yes, I can do that. I have six friends who will be happy to help. I'll have them come to the funeral. Do they need to wear any special clothes or anything? Good! No, sir, Miss Meadows was going to ask the pastor of her church, but I haven't spoken to her about it yet. I will be talking to her tomorrow. That's very good, sir, and I thank you very much," said Sarah as she placed the phone back in its cradle.

Sarah turned to Hannah, who was standing still in the doorway. "That was Blue Ridge Funeral Home. Margie has the funeral set for one o'clock Saturday. They want me to get six pall bearers, and I can get some of Tony's friends to do that. We only need to know if Margie contacted the preacher at her church. We can ask her when we go to the hospital, if she is able to talk to us."

"She got the pastor at her church. I thought I told you, Sarah. She called me yesterday or the day before . . . So much has happened that I can't keep things straight."

Hannah closed her eyes tightly for a moment, determined not to allow the threatening tears to pass through. She clinched her jaws together and murmured, "Well, let's finish breakfast and then go see Margie."

They pulled into the hospital parking lot at nine-thirty that morning. Sarah and Hannah walked from the car to the portico over the hospital entrance. Sarah stopped and, looking at

Hannah who looked so pale, asked "Are you all right, Hannah, I can get a wheelchair for you if you want me to."

Hannah straightened her shoulders and took a deep breath. "No, I'll not ride a wheelchair. I'm not a cripple. I just haven't gained all my strength back yet."

They went into the lobby and found a seat so Hannah could rest a few minutes. "Why don't you sit here and let me get the flowers you wanted to take to her. You wanted yellow roses, didn't you?" When Hannah nodded, Sarah walked hurriedly away down the corridor. She soon returned with the roses in cellophane wrapping. Then she walked beside of Hannah until they reached the elevators. Keith had said that Margie was in room 214 and they were soon outside the door.

Sarah tapped on the door and a woman's head peeped out of the crack in the door. "Oh! You must be Sarah. Margie was hoping you would come," and then looking at Hannah, the woman said, "You must be Hannah. Come in, both of you." She opened the door wider.

A very pale Margie sat propped up in the bed with a lunch tray in front of her.

"Hannah," she gasped. "You shouldn't have tried to come down here. You're not strong enough to be out yet."

Hannah came and hugged her as she said, "Yes, I am. You told me I had to be strong." She sat down by the bed and Sarah brought the flowers around with a flourish.

"These are for you, Miss Margie. We hope you like roses," said Sarah, presenting the flowers and kissing her cheek.

Margie burst into tears, and Jill hurried to her side. "Now, Margie, you promised you wouldn't get upset."

Margie smiled. "I'm not upset, Jill. These are happy tears. My family came and brought me roses."

Jill looked at Hannah and she also had tears in her eyes but wore a happy smile as did Sarah, whose eyes were misty, too.

Margie introduced Jill, and soon they were all talking calmly. "I think I'll get to go home today, Hannah." Margie sat toying with her food and keeping her lips clamped together, but she finally gained enough control to talk.

"Before I found out about . . . James, I called the Blue Ridge Funeral Home and the funeral is set for one o'clock Saturday. Did they call you?" asked Margie.

Sarah told her about the phone call, assuring her that she would get six of her son's friends to be pall bearers.

The doctor came through the door and stopped in amazement. "Miss Meadows, I told you not to get over stimulated and you've been crying." He turned to glare at the occupants of the room.

"Doctor, this is my family and they have just arrived. I'm crying because these are the first roses I ever received in my life," said Margie, trying to smile through her tears.

"I didn't know you had any family, Miss Meadows. That's what we were told by your friend, Miss Dawson," said the doctor.

Margie began crying again. "I adopted these people. This woman," she pointed to Hannah, "is my adopted daughter of the heart, but I don't have any real family, and now I don't even have James."

"Were you . . . I mean did you have a relationship with Mr. Harrison?" asked the doctor.

Margie glared at the doctor through her tears. "What do you mean? I loved James, but he didn't love me and we were not having an affair. He was good to me, though. He was better to me than anyone else in my life has ever been."

"We can't have you getting upset again. I'm going to have the nurse give you something to calm you," the doctor said and quickly left the room.

Jill, Hannah, and Sarah stood quietly looking at Margie until she said, "I'm going to be all right. James is gone and I can't change that. It hurts, but I've lived with worse." Margie shivered violently and looked at Hannah. "There are worse things than death, Hannah, but I hope you never have to experience them."

CHAPTER 21

"JILL, HURRY OUT THERE AND CATCH that doctor. I don't want or need any medication," urged Margie. Jill Dawson went out into the hall. This left Margie alone with Hannah and Sarah. She motioned for both of them to come close to the bed.

Almost whispering, she said, "I need to talk to you two, but since Jill works for Sam Henson I'm afraid to talk in front of her. I trust her, but Sam is a devious devil and he may wriggle something out of her."

Hannah and Sarah didn't know what to say, but Jill saved them by coming back into the room. "Margie, I just talked to the doctor and he's going to give you something mild. He said you would be all right alone, so I think I'll go home. I need a bath."

Margie smiled. "I really appreciate you staying with me, Jill, and I certainly hope it doesn't cause you a problem with Sam."

Jill shook her head. "It won't. Besides, I called in and told one of the office girls to give Sam a message. I'm surprised he didn't call here to check on you, even though he usually has me to do things like that."

Jill left with the warning that Margie had better not get upset again since they had aerobics on Monday. Margie swallowed her tears and reached for the Kleenex on the table beside her bed. Wiping her eyes, she retorted, "I'll be home before that."

She hadn't been gone long enough for Margie to talk to Hannah and Sarah before the nurse came in. "Miss Meadows, the doctor ordered this pill for you. It won't knock you out, but it will calm you," she said as she handed Margie the little cup with the pill in it and poured her a glass of water.

"What is it?" asked Margie, looking into the cup.

"It is Ativan, a mild nerve medication," explained the nurse.

Margie turned the cup up and swallowed the pill along with the water. "Now I'll be calm all night," said Margie as she tried to smile.

The nurse patted her on the arm and left the room. Margie turned to Sarah. "Close the door, Sarah. I have a lot to tell you."

Sarah shut the door and then came back to sit on the foot of Margie's bed.

"Did Keith tell you about James's will?" Margie had to stop for tears were drenching her face and she had trouble talking.

Finally gaining control, she grasped Hannah's hand. "James left most of what he had to me. He must have cared for me to do that; wouldn't you think so, Hannah?" Margie asked as if she wanted reassurance.

Hannah patted her hand and agreed that James probably really cared for her. Margie dried her eyes again and continued. "The other letter named the person he thought murdered Bill, but I can't say anything about that yet. In fact, Keith McCauley asked me to not reveal the contents of the letter to anyone until the trial. I just wanted to tell you. I knew it would ease your mind about Freddie being charged. Keith told me he would take care of everything, and so did Steve Hammer. I believe they will. I gave Keith the other letter, but he made a copy and brought the original back to me."

"That should be enough evidence to arrest the other person, shouldn't it?" asked Sarah.

"Margie, Sarah found a folder that Bill must have brought home that night he . . . died." Hannah had to stop. She clinched her jaws together and Sarah saw it.

She poured Hannah some water from the carafe on Margie's table. "Here, Hannah, drink this water and I'll tell Margie what we found."

Sarah explained to Margie about the short orders every three months and that all of them were signed by a Bertram Briscoll.

Margie gasped and shivered. "So he was working with Sam. You just don't know who to trust, do you?"

Sarah started to ask if Margie knew Briscoll, but stopped when the door opened. Keith, Steve, and another man with a briefcase came through the door.

"Well, nice people do tend to congregate, don't they?" Keith said and smiled at Hannah.

Hannah dropped her head. "We've only been here a little while. We were just ready to leave." Hannah rose from her chair, but quickly sat back down as the room started to rotate.

Seeing her extreme pallor, Sarah started to get up, but Hannah took a deep breath and shook her head. "I'm all right. It was just a momentary dizziness. I feel better now."

Keith put his hand on her shoulder. "I think you'd better sit there a few minutes longer, Mrs. Larkin. We don't want to have to put you to bed."

The man with the briefcase was introduced to Hannah as James Harrison's lawyer, Jerome Judson. Hannah knew that he was also the lawyer who was getting the bail bond hearing for Freddie. Hannah shook his hand and thanked him for his help.

Then Hannah and Sarah got up again, with Sarah holding onto Hannah's arm, and started out of the room. Keith was holding the door open when Sarah stopped. Talking quietly she said "Keith we found something at the house that we think you should have. Can you come over this evening?"

Keith assured them that he would. "It might be late."

"It's all right. We sometimes stay up until eleven or sometimes later. We'll still be up at ten o'clock, so don't worry about that."

"I'll try to be there before ten, but I'll call if I can't make it. Is that all right with you, Mrs. Larkin?" asked Keith.

Hannah nodded in agreement and walked to the elevators with Sarah still holding her arm. By the time she got to the car, she was so weak she was trembling. Sarah looked at her worriedly.

"Hannah, I shouldn't have let you come out. You aren't really able for all of this. I don't know what I was thinking," she said abjectly.

Hannah patted her arm. "I'll be all right, Sarah, as soon as I get home and take my medicine. Let's just go on home."

She wasn't all right when she got home, though, for when Sarah opened the door and flipped on the light Hannah felt uneasy. Then when Sarah opened the glass doors that led from the foyer into the living room, she knew why she had felt uneasy. They stepped into what had been a neat gracious room not two hours before and now the place was a wreck. Every drawer was pulled out, the cushions were on the floor, and the sofa was turned bottom up, as were the chairs.

Hannah had been behind Sarah and when she saw the room she gasped and clutched Sarah's arm. "Who . . . Sarah, somebody has destroyed my house!"

Sarah lifted one of the chairs into an upright position and Hannah sank gratefully into it. "That's right, Hannah. You sit right there, while I call Keith."

"Sarah, I'm going to the bedroom. I'll bet they were looking for that folder." Sarah followed Hannah into the bedroom, which was also a shambles. Drawers were hanging open and the bed was stripped. The mattress was half off the frame. When Hannah tried to pull the drawer of the dresser on out she was shaking so badly that Sarah said, "Here, Hannah let me do that."

Sarah pulled the drawer completely out and Hannah said, "You have to turn it bottom up, Sarah. After I showed you what I had found I was still uneasy. I don't know why, but I wanted to make sure it was safe, so I taped it to the bottom of that drawer. Lift the drawer up and see if the folder is still on the bottom."

The folder was still there, and Hannah let out a sigh of relief. "You'd better call Keith before somebody else decides to come and search again," murmured Hannah weakly and she sat down on the box springs of the bed. While Sarah made the call from the phone on the nightstand, Hannah tried to muster all her strength.

In an effort to strengthen her resolve Hannah chided herself. "Daddy used to say, 'You're going to have to be stronger than this, Hannah, so get a stiff upper lip. Life ain't easy but you have to live it anyway.'"

CHAPTER 22

KEITH RECEIVED THE CALL FROM SARAH and quickly called Steve. "Steve, the Larkin home has been ransacked. No, it was like that when Hannah and Sarah reached home after their visit to see Margie," Keith explained.

"I'll have to meet you there, Keith, but I'm on my way."

Sarah didn't move anything, since she thought the police might want to take pictures. "Hannah, I'm so proud that you had the foresight to really hide that folder," she said as she sank to the floor beside the one upright chair in the living room where Hannah was sitting. Hannah would have given the chair to Sarah but she knew Sarah would refuse it.

"Sarah, do you suppose Sam Henson did this? I can't imagine a business man who has his position doing something like this, can you?" asked Hannah.

"He could have hired someone, but we just don't know. There's so many things happening since Bill died that it just boggles my mind," Sarah replied, frowning in puzzlement.

"I think I'll make some coffee if they haven't torn the stove to shreds," said Hannah, rising from her seat.

Sarah rose to her feet. "No, you sit right back down. I'll make the coffee."

By the time Keith and Steve arrived, Sarah had brought two cups of freshly brewed coffee to the living room. She had just handed Hannah her cup when the doorbell rang.

Keith and Steve walked in and stared in astonishment. "Somebody wanted something, and it appears they were in a hurry to find it," said Steve. Keith followed him from room to room. The living room and bedroom were in worse shape than the others, but none were left untouched.

"I don't suppose you've checked to see if anything is missing, have you?" Steve asked Hannah.

"No, I haven't because I think I know what they were looking for." She pulled the folder from behind her back and handed it to Keith.

Steve stepped to Keith's side and they stood looking through the folder as the pages were slowly turned. Suddenly Keith stopped. "Oh yes, this is what they were looking for all right. Look at this, Steve. Looks like Bertie Briscoll signed his own warrant."

Soon two investigators arrived and began their meticulous picture taking, lifting of fingerprints, and clue searching. Keith had locked the folder Hannah had given him in the glove compartment of his car before the investigators arrived, so they went away not having any idea why the house had been vandalized.

As they left, Keith told Sarah to keep all the doors and windows locked and should anything suspicious occur, to give him a call. "I don't care what hour it is. Since they didn't find what they wanted they may come back."

Sarah agreed to call and said, "I'm surprised they didn't ransack Bill's car." Her eyes opened wide. "I didn't look! I'm going to the garage."

Sarah almost ran toward the garage with Keith and Steve right behind her. The side door was standing open. Bill's silver El Dorado had its seats slashed, and everything in the glove compartment was out on the floor. The men walked all around the car shaking their heads.

"Well, we know for sure that they wanted something they thought Mr. Larkin had left here, and we know they came through the garage." Steve said as they turned back to the kitchen.

"It almost looks like this was done by somebody who knew Mr. Larkin pretty well," said Keith as he pointed out that the living room, the kitchen, the master bedroom, and Mr. Larkin's car had the most damage.

"They can't blame this on Freddie since he's still in jail," said Hannah with malice in her voice.

Keith clapped Hannah on the shoulder. "No, H . . . uh, Mrs. Larkin, your son is definitely not a suspect. I have a pretty good idea who did this or who hired someone else to do it, don't you Steve?"

Steve rolled his eyes and nodded. "Yep, I'm afraid I do, and it isn't a pretty picture.

Sarah watched the two men and thought, "These two know something that is troubling both of them and I wonder what it is?"

Before the men left, they told Hannah and Sarah they would be at the church on Saturday for the funeral.

They also offered help with the arrangements. Hannah thanked them both, but said she thought everything was already arranged. "Margie arranged everything before Mr. Harrison died."

"Hannah, how long have you known Margie Meadows?" Steve asked.

"Bill introduced me to Margie over twenty years ago, when I was expecting Freddie. I never got to know her until Bill died, though. Since then she has been like a mother to me. In fact, she sent flowers every day that I was in the hospital, when I was so sick."

Keith had stood thoughtfully listening. "I thought she was a close relative. In fact you all act as if you are closely related." He grinned. "You sure could've fooled me."

As Steve and Keith drove back to the station, Steve said, "If Prosecutor Swann gets a sealed indictment, I think the judge should set a trial date, don't you?"

"I hope he will. I think some fur is going to fly in that courtroom," Keith replied.

"I doubt if the chief will agree with us. I hope we'll find out what went down between him and Sam Henson's lawyer, don't you?" asked Steve.

"I'll bet a trial will bring a lot of things to light that the chief hasn't wanted checked too closely. He's not really tried to stop us, but he's certainly pushed us to arrest some people, while he's not been too happy when we've arrested others," replied Keith.

Steve's eyebrows rose. "Like not mentioning a need to arrest Mr. Briscoll? He may have his reasons, but it was certainly a different story when he wanted Freddie arrested."

They drove along, each thinking about the case. They now knew that poison had been used on Bill Larkin and Sabrina Draper. She was still in intensive care in the hospital. They knew that James Harrison was dead but were not certain of the reason except that Sam Henson had threatened to reveal something that Harrison didn't want known. Sam Henson was also involved in the whole mess. Freddie Larkin had been held as a suspect in the murder of Bill Larkin, but neither of them believed he was guilty.

Steve blew out an exasperated breath. "You're right, Keith. The only way to really know is to set the trial and see what is revealed. There's enough circumstantial evidence to make a lot of people nervous."

"So far, Thomas Mitchell and Hannah Larkin seem to be the only people free of suspicion," said Keith.

"Margie Meadows isn't under suspicion unless you know something that I don't," stated Steve.

"No, I'm not really suspicious of her, but I do wonder why James Harrison suddenly changed his will and left everything under her control." Keith muttered.

"Well, we don't know who was named before he changed his will, but that doesn't make me suspicious of Margie. I just wonder about James Harrison's motive. He was too shrewd not to have a reason for his actions," replied Steve.

CHAPTER 23

Since it was now only eight-thirty Steve and Keith swung by the hospital and asked about Sabrina Draper. The doctor came out to talk to them. "She is gradually getting better physically, but we have no idea what this has done to her mentally until she is fully awake. I wish she had someone to sit and talk to her. Sometimes that helps coma patients," explained the doctor.

Both men left the hospital depressed. Using drugs was bad enough, without being poisoned. "Thomas Mitchell said he didn't know where she obtained the cocaine, but I felt he knew more than he was telling," said Steve.

"That's why I think we should get some of these people under oath. I know people perjure themselves, but they're more apt to get caught up in a court trial," replied Keith.

They pulled into the station as the chief came out the door. He stopped when he saw them. "That Judge Wilson has granted a sealed indictment. It's too soon. We don't have all the information we need. It makes it damn inconvenient," he spat out in disgust.

Keith looked at Steve. "We were just hoping the date would be set, Chief. It will help us to tie all the ends together," said Steve.

"What ends? We know that Freddie Larkin's fingerprints were all over the glass that had poison in it, and that Sam

Henson is in jail because of James Harrison's statements. That's it. There are no loose ends. We don't have proof of anything," stormed Chief Donaldson.

"Well, we have a few more things for you to think about. Bill Larkin's home was broken into today. It seems somebody is trying to find something they think he had," Steve replied.

Keith added, "Steve and I have been looking at all the angles of this case and we think the judge made a really wise move."

"Humph! That's not the way I see it. What about that Draper woman? We don't know what she knows, and since she'll probably never be able to tell us anything I think there are angles that still need to be checked before any trials are held."

"What date did he set?" asked Steve. He didn't want to argue with the chief.

"Next Thursday, which gives us less than a week to get . . . gather everything together. How is the Draper woman doing?" asked the chief.

Steve looked at Keith and then proceeded to tell Donaldson what the doctor had told them. The chief seemed to be so relieved that his shoulders slumped.

"That's too bad. She probably knows a lot of the shenanigans of the people with CEE. She's worked with almost every one of the big boys," he said and grinned before he finished with, "in one way or another."

Steve and Keith stepped past the chief and Keith said, "I guess we may as well call it quits for today. Steve and I plan to attend Bill Larkin's funeral. It's tomorrow at one o'clock. I want permission to take Freddie Larkin to his father's funeral. Will you approve of that?" Keith looked at the chief in speculation.

"Sure, that's all right. Judson has already been in my office three times to work that out."

"Will you be at the funeral, Chief?" Steve Hammer asked.

The chief shook his head. "No, I never met the man. I have several angles I want to check on anyway. Will you be coming by here in the morning?"

"We need to talk to Margie Meadows again, and we also want to talk to James Harrison's lawyer, Jerome Judson. We may talk to some other people too, so we may not make it in" said Steve over his shoulder as he opened the door.

"Well, good night. I'll see you two on Monday."

The two men went in and checked for messages. They were ready to walk out the door when the phone rang. "Beckley police station, Sergeant Keith McCauley speaking," said Keith and quickly drew in his breath.

"Calm down, Margie. We'll be there in about ten minutes," Keith assured her, and hung up the phone.

He turned to Steve, "Jill Dawson just drove Margie home and somebody has broken into Margie's place also."

Steve clamped his jaws together angrily. "What did they think Margie had? She didn't work with Bill Larkin. Let's get out there before she has to go back to the hospital. She's too sick to have to deal with anything else right now."

The men pulled into Margie's parking lot nine minutes later and soon were ringing her doorbell. Jill opened the door. "Come in. Maybe you two can calm Margie down. To tell you the truth, this shocked me too." The men stepped into the room and gasped in shock. Margie's beautiful apartment was ruined. Furniture was broken and scattered, pictures were slashed, statues broken, and even the carpet was pulled up. Jill had brought a chair from the kitchen and Margie was huddled in it shaking as if she had palsy.

Fearing she would have to go back to the hospital, Steve knelt in front of her. "Have you taken any nerve medicine?"

"No, she hasn't. I just got her in the door and we saw this mess. She was so torn up over her paintings that I had to almost drag her to the chair," said Jill tiredly.

"Well, get one of her pills, Jill. She needs to take something or she'll have to go right back to the hospital," said Steve.

Keith had been wandering around the apartment. He came back into the living room. "It looks like they became angry when they couldn't find anything and just tried to destroy everything they could."

In the meantime, Steve had gotten Margie to swallow a pill and stood beside her. "I guess we should get the lab over here. Do you want me to call?" he asked.

Keith nodded and Steve went looking for the phone. When he found it, there was no dial tone. The cord had been jerked from the wall. "It's a good thing we have cell phones. This phone won't be any benefit for a good while."

Keith came over and patted Margie on the shoulder. "I think you should let Jill pack you some clothes so Steve and I can take you to a hotel."

Margie shivered. "I need to go to Hannah and Sarah. I want to attend Bill's funeral. Just take me to their house. They have been begging me to move in with them, anyway."

Keith didn't think she was in any shape to attend a funeral, but he liked the idea of her going to Hannah's house. "We'll take you. Should we call first?" he asked.

Margie nodded before she turned to Jill and asked for help in packing her clothes. Jill held Margie's arm and they moved cautiously through the tangled mess of broken furniture and statuary toward the bedroom. Steve brought a chair to the bedroom so Margie could sit down while she directed the packing.

Keith had just finished his call to Hannah when the crime scene investigators arrived and began their routine. He went into the bedroom and informed Margie that Hannah was delighted that she wanted to come to them.

"Their house was broken into as well, Margie, but the neighbors came in and have the mess cleared up," he explained.

"Somebody must think that Bill had something hidden at their house, but I can't understand who might have thought I had anything," said Margie tearfully.

Steve was standing behind Margie's chair. "I think someone knows that you have letters from James Harrison that may implicate them, Margie," he said as he patted her on the shoulder.

Margie sat thinking about this while she shook her head yes or no to the things Jill was folding to place in her suitcase. "How many people know that I received letters, Steve? I know you, Keith, Chief Donaldson, Jerome Judson, Jill, and . . ."

"Sam Henson," interrupted Jill. "I didn't think anyone would care if I told Sam, since he is one of the partners in CEE," she explained.

"I didn't tell him what was in the letters since I didn't know, anyway," she finished, looking uneasy.

"When did you see Sam?" asked Keith.

"When I came home yesterday afternoon, I called to tell Sam I would be back to work Monday. I didn't get him, but

Peggy Stevens was working and I talked to her. CEE is closed until after the funerals so I don't really know why she was there. Anyway, she said she'd see that Sam got my message. About an hour later Sam called me. He wanted to know what happened to Margie, and I told him about the letters. Sam wouldn't do this. He's an old man, and this had to be done by somebody strong."

Knowing that Sam was in jail, neither Keith nor Steve made any comment, but Margie said, "I know he's your boss, Jill, but I don't trust Sam Henson. I never have."

Jill shrugged her shoulders. "You used to. You got me the job working for him, Margie, but whether you trust him or not, he's not strong enough to do the damage done here."

CHAPTER 24

Steve and Keith drove Margie to Pike Lane, where she settled into Hannah's spare bedroom. Sarah and Hannah's other neighbors had brought in food. Now, they all sat around Hannah's dining table as Sarah served them.

While they were eating, Keith filled Sarah and Hannah in on the condition of Margie's house.

"Coming to stay with us is now out of your hands, isn't it, Margie?" Sarah asked, smiling at Margie.

Hannah, seated beside Margie, patted her hand. "I'm sure Margie didn't want her house torn up to enable her to come to us, Sarah."

Margie looked around with eyes brimming with tears. "My beautiful paintings that James bought for me are ruined. I had some nice furniture, but that didn't mean as much to me as those paintings."

Steve finished chewing soberly. "I'll bet a good art restorer could put them back, just like they were. Don't you think they could, Keith?" he asked.

"There's a new place on Dry Hill Road, right off Harper Road in that new strip mall. Somebody mentioned their work the other day. I can't remember much of what they said except that some of their restored work was on display at Tamarack," replied Keith.

"Well, as soon as the funeral is over and I get a little strength back, I'll take them out there and see," Margie said hopefully.

"I could run by your place and pick them up this evening and take them out there tomorrow morning," offered Steve.

Margie was pleased. Before they left, she gave Steve the key to her place. "I'll see what else can be salvaged while I'm there," he promised as he left.

The members of the Larkin household were up early the morning of the funeral, but both Margie and Hannah had to almost force themselves to move about.

"Margie, I feel like I'm ninety years old this morning. I hope I don't look as bad as I feel," Hannah complained.

"If you girls feel like ninety, how do you think I feel? Maybe the nerve medication you both are on right now is causing you both to feel dragged out?" said Sarah.

They discussed medicines and agreed that as soon as life settled down they both intended never to take nerve medicine again.

"Well, I won't unless I should lose Freddie, Sarah, or you, Margie," said Hannah slowly.

Together, the women made toast, eggs, and sausage but only Sarah cleaned her plate. "You two get in there and start getting prettied up. I'll clean up the dishes," she ordered.

At twelve-thirty Keith and Steve pulled up in front of the Larkin residence. When Hannah saw Freddie step from the backseat tears blinded her eyes.

"There's Freddie. They've gotten him out for the funeral. Oh thank the Good Lord."

Freddie was soon wrapped in the arms of his mother, while two other women patted his back and gazed at him from loving eyes. The two officers weren't even noticed for several minutes.

Suddenly Sarah stepped back and gasped. "I'm sorry, fellows, that you're being ignored, but right now Freddie is the star of this show."

Before any comments were made the phone rang and Sarah answered. Those present could hear the joy in Sarah's voice. "Sure, Tony, you know I will. I was going to Hannah's husband's funeral, but her son is here now, so I don't think I'll be needed." Sarah hung up and turned with a smile on her face. "Tony is on his way and wants me to go with him to Florida for a visit."

Hannah put her arms around Sarah. "Oh Sarah, I'm so glad. You've missed him so much. I'll miss you but we are also happy for you, so go on and enjoy yourself."

Sarah gave everyone a radiant smile. "All of you be good to Hannah until I get back or you'll answer to me." She turned and did a jaunty trot upstairs to collect her things.

Once Sarah left, Freddie escorted the two women to the car and ushered them into the back seat before he climbed in beside them. Freddie reached up and tapped Keith on the shoulder. "You may proceed to the church, Jeeves."

Keith grinned. "Now, I'm elevated to chauffeur status, I guess. Sometimes, I wish that's all I had to do."

At the church, Freddie walked between Hannah and Margie as they climbed the steps. There they were met by the ushers and escorted into the sanctuary. Going down the aisle, Hannah noted that several people she had met with CEE were present. She nodded and smiled. When they were seated, people began to come by to express their sympathy.

"This doesn't seem real, does it, Freddie?" asked Hannah.

Freddie shook his head and started to say something else when the preacher mounted the pulpit and the organ began. The preacher talked about the record Bill Larkin had left behind of being honest, hardworking, a good father and husband, and about how much he would be missed.

The lid of the casket was closed and remained that way until the service ended. Then the funeral director lifted the lid and the mourners passed by, stopping to speak to Hannah and Freddie.

Margie had sat very still all during the entire procedure and Hannah had managed to remain dry-eyed during the entire service. Once in a while she heard a muffled sniff coming from Margie. Hannah wondered at this, but thought Margie was just weak and the funeral made it worse.

The funeral director came to lead the family past the body for one last time, and it was then that Hannah broke down. She just couldn't get the image of Bill lying in a pool of blood on her living room floor out of her head. Now, however, he looked like the Bill she had married and loved for over twenty years. She felt she couldn't let him go, but knew she had to.

I have to let him go. He'd been acting like he didn't want to be with me for the past two years and now he'll be away forever, she thought as she placed her hand on Bill's chest and whispered her good-bye so softly that only Freddie and Keith heard her. She thought she had cried all her sorrow out, but now she found her face awash in tears and her body trembling all over. Keith McCauley, who had positioned himself beside her and Freddie, placed his hand beneath her elbow as she started to move on. She leaned against him.

Freddie's face had lost all color. "Dad, Dad," he whispered. "I did love you. I truly did," he said and staggered as he walked beside of Hannah. They heard a sound and turned to see Margie Meadows trembling and she had covered her face with her hands. Steve Hammer stepped to her side and slipped his arm around her shoulders. With his support Margie walked haltingly toward the door toward the waiting car.

Keith, Hannah and Freddie brought up the rear and soon everyone was in the car again but this time Steve sat holding Margie against his chest with Hannah on the other side and Freddie in the front with Keith. Soon their car was in the long line behind the hearse that wove its way along Robert C. Byrd Drive toward Sophie, West Virginia.

When they reached the cemetery, Keith got out with Hannah and Freddie but Steve remained in the car with Margie. Walking between Freddie and Keith, Hannah made it to the gravesite and sank gratefully on to the prepared seat with the two men on each side of her. When the preacher came to the part "ashes to ashes and dust to dust" Hannah knew she was to sprinkle the grave. She slowly reached down, picked up some of the red clay, and crumbled it into her hand. Supported by Keith and Freddie, she leaned over and managed to sift the dust onto the casket.

I'm so weak that I just know I can't make it to the car, thought Hannah and tried to think of the way Bill had treated her for the past two or three years. She hoped anger would make her strong. It helped some but she was still trembling.

Keith McCauley looked at Freddie who was also very upset and really not paying much attention to his mother. He was trying to control his own grief. Making a quick decision Keith put his arm around Hannah's waist to support her as she stood to leave the cemetery. In this way the three of them made their way to the car and Hannah was helped into the front seat.

Margie had revived and now wanted to help Hannah. She leaned over the back of the seat. "Hannah, are you all right?"

Hannah looked back at Margie. "I'm a little shaky, but I'm all right. I'll be a lot better when I get home though. How are you feeling?"

Margie smiled tiredly. "I feel more like wet spaghetti than anything else. Is it over? If it is, then like you, I'd like to go home."

When they arrived back at Hannah's they found the neighbors were there waiting. A pretty blond woman came to meet them with a smile. "Come on in and grab a seat and we'll serve the food."

What looked like a feast for a king was spread out enticingly on the kitchen table and counter top. Margie looked amazed. "Wow, you really have good neighbors, don't you, Hannah?"

Hannah smiled. "I certainly do and I thank each of you for all you've done. I'll try to return the favor, but not for something like this I hope."

"We don't need any thanks, but we certainly don't want to carry this food away, so come on and eat," said the next door neighbor, Priscilla Dale, and patted Hannah's shoulder gently.

Soon everyone was seated with a plate of food and most of the neighbors had left. Before she left, Priscilla told Keith that a car had made several trips by the house. "Whoever it was drove very slowly, as if he was looking to see if anyone was here."

"Did you note the make and color of the car? We might be able to trace it if you did." Steve sat waiting.

Priscilla shook her head. "I know it was an old green car, rusted out in places, but honestly I don't know a Chevrolet from a Ford."

"That's all right, for at least this puts us on the alert," said Keith, looking at Steve for agreement.

Both Margie and Hannah perked up at the word 'alert.' "Do you think someone will come back to search the house again?" asked Margie.

"They might, but don't worry, girls. We'll put a stakeout around your house for a few nights," Keith promised and turned to look at Steve narrowly.

"Better still, I'll stay until two a.m. and then Steve will come and take over. If anyone should call don't say a word about any of this, not even to Jill, Margie."

Hannah shook her head. "We can't ask you two to do this. You have more important things to do, and it might cause you some trouble. Besides, we can each take turns staying awake ourselves."

"We usually have Sundays off anyway, unless we have an urgent case. Nobody will know that we are doing this," stated Steve.

"None of you need to stay awake. All of you are worn out, even Freddie, but he will be safe in jail for a few more days. We will be taking turns watching. Is there some place we could hide the car?"

Seeing that their minds were made up, Freddie told them to park the car behind Sarah's house. "I'll call her and tell her what you plan to do. She'll be glad since she seemed worried," replied Freddie.

CHAPTER 25

AFTER RETURNING FREDDIE TO THE JAIL, Keith took the first watch as they had planned, and the occupants of the house slept soundly. Steve showed up at two the next morning and parked his car behind Sarah's house as Keith pulled out. For the next hour all was quiet. Steve had just opened his thermos and poured a cup of coffee when a car crept slowly down the street. Steve's position was hidden at the side of the house shielded by a crape myrtle bush. When the car eased to a stop, Steve hit the button on his cell phone to alert Keith. Soon he saw two men walking stealthily up the street toward where he was hidden. One was carrying a large container and as they got nearer Steve realized that it was a five-gallon can.

The man stopped and set it down. He swung his arm back and forth. "Damn, that's heavy," he muttered softly, rubbing his arm. The other man stopped beside him.

"Here, let me have that. You'll drop the damn can. We don't want it spilled. We have to use it, you stupid jerk," he scolded, just as Steve stepped out with his gun drawn.

"Put your hands over your heads and back away from that can," he ordered.

The men jerked in surprise and the first man stepped backward against the can, knocking it over. The smell of gasoline permeated the air and his partner cursed.

Just at that moment Keith's car pulled into the driveway. In the headlights the two would-be arsonists were revealed. Keith got out of the car and walked up to them.

"Well hello, boys. How many more times are you two going to let somebody talk you into doing their dirty work?" Keith asked, since he knew both men.

"I don't know what you're talking about," snarled the taller of the two.

"Oh yes you do, Robert Stallard. You broke into Margie Meadows's apartment yesterday, and here you are with a gas can at two-thirty in the morning," said Keith.

"How did you know we broke into the Meadows apartment?" blurted Stallard's partner.

"Shut up, stupid. He don't know nothing, so just shut up," ordered Stallard.

Steve turned to the other man. "What's your name? You may as well tell us, since we're going to take you down to the station and they'll get it anyway."

"He's Buddy Gibson. He's the one they get to do their dirty work, aren't you Buddy?" asked Keith quietly.

Buddy recognized Keith and stuttered. "I'll bet if the ch . . ." he didn't get to finish since Stallard slammed his fist into the side of his jaw.

Steve grabbed Stallard's arm and wrenched it behind his back so hard he cursed. "Don't break my damn arm, man!"

Keith caught Buddy and handcuffed him while Steve did the same to Stallard. They marched the men to Keith's car with Steve's gun aimed at them. They were soon installed in the back seat with Steve keeping his eyes and gun trained on them from the front seat.

When they arrived at the station, their friend Sergeant Dave Shortt was on duty. Keith didn't want Donaldson to know about the arrest, because Buddy Gibson had a broken jaw from almost saying what they suspected to be the chief's name. He explained the situation to David Shortt and requested that the two men be incarcerated in one of the upstairs cells. When Keith asked this he looked at Dave, lifted his eyebrows and nodded. Dave grinned. "I understand, old buddy."

As Sergeant Shortt marched the two handcuffed men through the heavy doors in the rear he gave Keith a knowing wink.

The two officers went back to their car as Steve said, "I think I'd better go back and get that gasoline can and bring it in for evidence. I think I'll finish out my shift before I bring it back, though."

Keith agreed that he was probably wise to finish his stakeout time. "If one of the women should wake up expecting us to be there and one of us wasn't there, they would probably get upset."

Keith took Steve back, but once there, they decided that Keith should retrieve the gasoline can. He went home leaving Steve to finish his stint.

"I'll check in around eight o'clock in the morning," Keith promised as he pulled away.

When Margie came out to get the paper the next morning, she found Steve sitting on the porch steps drinking coffee.

"Good morning! I hope I didn't wake you girls last night. I tried to be quiet," Steve yawned.

"Did you sit on those steps all night?" asked Margie as she plucked the paper from the paper box and turned back to the steps.

"No, I didn't do much sitting around last night," Steve said with a smile as he followed Margie into the house.

When they were inside Steve told Margie about the arrest.

"They were planning to burn us alive, weren't they? What kind of person would deliberately burn people, alive or dead? Could those papers Bill brought home be that important?" asked Margie, shivering in revulsion.

"Steve wiped his hand across his face. "I don't have the answer to that, Margie, but we may find out Thursday, and it can't be too soon for me."

"That's the same day as Freddie's hearing. Can they have two trials on the same day?" asked Margie.

"Freddie's is a hearing, Margie, which is about whether or not he should be bound over to the Grand Jury, but Sam Henson is already indicted," explained Steve.

Then their talk turned to Hannah, Freddie, and the funeral. "I thought more of the people Bill worked with would show up at his funeral, but not many did," said Margie.

"Actually several were there, Margie. I saw Thomas Mitchell and his family, Henson's wife and daughter, and almost all of the secretaries and office workers. I saw Mr. Shrader, who runs the warehousing branch, there with his wife and son. I guess some of them were attending the ceremony for James Harrison. He was cremated yesterday, but I didn't want to tell you. Margie, are you . . . were you in love with him?" asked Steve.

Margie didn't answer and Steve feared he had offended her, but finally she said, "I don't know, but we never dated. Sometimes I thought he was going to ask me out, but he never did."

Steve thoughtfully let this sink in before he said, "I don't know if you could have been present at the cremation anyway, but you may have wanted to be. Maybe I should have told you, but you were so torn up over your apartment that I just didn't mention it."

"That's all right, Steve. You were probably right and I couldn't have been present anyway." She sat silent for a moment and then turned to look toward the stairs expecting Hannah to come down soon.

Steve sat wondering why Margie was so involved with Bill Larkin's family. Watching her actions around them he knew she really liked Hannah and Freddie. She acted like they were her family and they seemed to like it that way, but Steve realized that the relationship was rather unusual. Bill Larkin, as far as he knew, was only a co-worker with Margie.

Someday, I'm going to ask her. She'll have to give me some kind of answer, thought Steve.

Hannah came down the stairs. "Good, I was afraid you'd be gone," she said as she crossed the room to the coffee pot.

Steve had been busy watching Margie. He sat wondering why he was so attracted to her. She was short but not dumpy as most short women became as they aged. Her hair was still dark. She was attractive, but not beautiful like Hannah Larkin. He'd found her attractive when he first met her, but knew she only thought of him as a policeman doing his duty.

Hannah came to the table and sat down sipping from her cup. "Well, we're still safe and sound, so you must have done a good job last night."

"We'd better be glad he was here, Hannah. He arrested two men last night," Margie said as Hannah took the chair next to Margie.

"Were they trying to break into our house, again?" asked Hannah aghast.

"No. They were planning to burn our house."

Hannah put down her cup and caught hold of the table edges with both hands. "Were they planning to burn us alive? Oh my God!" She turned deathly pale.

Margie patted her hand that now lay limply on the table. "I shouldn't have blurted that out like that, Hannah. Relax and just thank Steve for being here. I just wanted you to know how much Steve and Keith have done for us."

Steve explained the entire episode, giving the women time to get over the initial shock. They both thanked him and told him to pass along their thanks to Keith.

Then Steve told Hannah about James Harrison's cremation and Margie who already knew, sat dry-eyed. She bit her lip and turned to Steve.

"Thanks, Steve, but don't worry. I wouldn't have wanted to go even if it had been allowed. James Harrison was the only man I had met in all my life who did things for people just because he had a good heart. He didn't expect anything in return, and I loved him for it, but I was not in love with James. He was just a very honest, generous man and I'll miss him."

CHAPTER 26

Since it was Sunday, the Larkin household stayed at home and relaxed. Margie seemed very satisfied to be there and Hannah felt happy to have her there, but they both missed Sarah Preston. Jill Dawson called to check on Margie and even though she was pleased that Jill called, she didn't mention the attempted arson.

"Margie, do you think the judge will discover who really killed Bill and who poisoned the Draper woman?" Hannah asked as she sipped the hot chocolate Margie had made.

"I hope they figure out that Freddie didn't do it. I know he's tired of being treated like a criminal."

They sat discussing the case, starting with Bill's death, Sabrina's poisoning, and James Harrison's death, the destruction of Margie's apartment, and Hannah's house, as well as the attempt to burn Hannah's house down. They were still talking when Margie switched on the television. The first thing they saw was Chief Donaldson being interviewed by a Channel Four reporter. They were not surprised when he said that Sam Henson had been arrested.

"I wonder when they arrested him. I didn't let the police read my letters, but I did give Keith and Steve a copy," Margie said, puzzled over some niggling remembrance.

"What is it Margie? Why are you frowning like that?" asked Hannah. Was there something in your letter that implicated Sam Henson?" she asked.

Margie stared at Hannah for a moment and then shook her head. "I'm not at liberty to say what was in my letter."

Still concentrating, she continued. "There's just something that sounds familiar about Chief Donaldson. I don't know what it is, but it is something."

Hannah assured her that she understood her having to keep the contents of her letter secret. She, however, made no comment about her thoughts on Chief Donaldson. They sat raptly listening to the rest of the interview with Donaldson. He seemed upset and kept saying that Henson was innocent until proven guilty and that the media should stress that.

"Sam Henson is an important business man in this area who would have no reason to be involved in any underhanded schemes."

Hannah had been thinking about what Keith and Steve had said about Sabrina Draper not having anyone. She said, "I think I'll call to see if I can go in and talk to Miss Draper."

Margie jerked around to stare at her. "You want to go talk to that woman. What do you want to talk to her about? You don't know her."

"Margie, she doesn't have anybody. Keith said the doctor wished that she had some family," stated Hannah.

"I don't think you are able yet, Hannah. Why don't you give yourself a few more days before you go out to help other people? Besides, I don't think she's allowed any visitors. I guess they won't allow any, because people are being killed and poisoned."

Steve called late that evening to see if they were all right. He told Margie that he had left two of her paintings with the shop that Keith had told them about. "The man said he thought he could restore them to almost their original state," he explained.

"How much did he say it would cost?" asked Margie.

Not wanting her to know, since he planned to pay for the work himself, Steve replied. "I didn't ask him. I was just so pleased to find someone to restore them for you, that I forgot to ask."

Margie thanked him and asked if Sam Henson had been arrested because of what was in her letters from James Harrison. Steve explained that Harrison had also written a letter to him and Henson's arrest was because of what was revealed in that letter.

The next three days were spent in a similar manner in the Larkin house. Hannah and Margie gained more strength and talked constantly.

"They talk as if they are sisters or a mother and daughter who have been separated for a long time and have just now been reunited," said Steve when he talked to Keith.

Thursday morning found Hannah and Margie up early, waiting for Steve to arrive. He had promised to escort them to the courthouse for Freddie's hearing, and they were ready when he pulled to a stop before their house. On the way, Margie wanted to know what things Steve had been doing.

"Keith and I have been checking every angle in this case and I've never seen a spider with a bigger web nor a more tangled one."

The two women were so nervous that they talked non-stop all the way and Steve grinned as he said, "I hope today will prove that Freddie is innocent, but if it does he may have to move in with me. With two women talking a mile a minute he'll be worn out in no time," he said, laughing nervously himself.

"Men talk just as much as women but they talk about things that women aren't interested in and women don't sit around and guzzle beer while they talk," countered Margie, giving Steve a cheeky grin.

When they arrived the courtroom was only partially filled, but Keith had still reserved two seats up near the front of the room for them. They were seated and sat waiting with everyone else for the judge to enter the chamber.

Soon the bailiff called, "All rise, Judge Nathan Wilson presiding." The judge, who was much younger than Hannah thought a judge would be, came slowly into the room and finally took his seat behind the bench.

When everyone was seated, Judge Wilson called the case of the State against Freddie Larkin to be presented. The state's attorney presented their witnesses, Sergeant Keith McCauley and Inspector Steve Hammer. Both men testified that Bill Larkin had been found dead in his living room, that Freddie Larkin was the last person to see him alive, and that the glass in which the poison was found was covered with the fingerprints of Freddie Larkin. Steve also stated that Nicole Henson had said that Freddie hated his father.

The judge ruled this to be enough evidence of probable cause to bind the case over to the Grand Jury for the next term of court. Freddie was told that he was still under bond, but that he could return home.

Freddie gave a sigh of relief as did Hannah and Margie who had remained seated, but were visibly shaken. Judson had warned them that this was likely to happen since witnesses were seldom called in a Grand Jury hearing.

Then the case of the State against Sam Henson was called to be presented and to everyone's surprise, the first witness the state attorney called was Margie Meadows.

Margie turned as white as a sheet of paper and had to be helped to the witness chair. After swearing Margie in, Kyle Swann, the prosecuting attorney, began asking for identification data. Margie went through her age, place of residence, where she worked and how long she had worked there. She felt some of the tension leave her since the questions seemed to be routine. The next question, however, brought her forward in her seat.

"Miss Meadows did you or did you not hire Jerome Judson to defend Freddie Larkin in this case?" asked Mr. Swann.

"No, sir, I did not hire Mr. Judson," she answered.

Mr. Swann's eyes glared for a moment. "Do you know who did hire Jerome Judson?"

"Yes, sir, I do know who hired him."

"Please tell the court who hired Mr. Judson, Miss Meadows."

"I asked James Harrison to tell me of a good lawyer and James Harrison hired Mr. Judson." Margie took a long drink of the water provided while Swann patiently waited. When she sat back he continued.

"Until Bill Larkin was found dead, had you ever met Freddie Larkin?"

"No, sir, I had not." Margie answered in a shaky voice.

"Are you telling me and this court that through your efforts the most expensive lawyer in this town was hired to defend a young man whom you had never met?"

Margie nodded, but dropped her head.

"Answer yes or no, Miss Meadows," ordered Swann.

"Yes, because Freddie Larkin is innocent. He didn't send that bottle of Mylanta to his dad. I did," said Margie, sobbing.

There were audible gasps as everyone in the courtroom perked up and sat forward in their seats.

"Why did you send tainted Mylanta to Bill Larkin, Miss Meadows?" asked Swann and stood waiting until Margie blew her nose and took a long breath.

"I can't answer that in just a yes or no," she said.

"That's fine, Miss Meadows. You take your time and tell the court how that came about," urged Swann.

"I'll try," said Margie in a breathy voice. "Sam Henson brought Mylanta to a stress reduction workshop that CEE was holding for its employees. Every participant was told they could take two bottles. I don't know if someone took more than two, or what happened, but when Sabrina Draper came to get hers none was left. I told the boy who helped Sam Henson bring the Mylanta in to go into the back and see if Sam had anymore and the boy left." Here Margie stopped and blew her nose again. She was not only ashen, but her hands were in constant movement either rubbing her face, her hair, or her ears.

"Did the boy bring Mylanta back to the conference, Miss Meadows?" asked Swann.

"Yes, but he gave it to me since I was waiting for it in the hall just outside the room," stated Margie with a wide-eyed stare.

"Why were you waiting for it in the hall instead of the conference room?" the prosecutor asked.

"I had gone back to the bathroom and . . . the walls between the two bathrooms must have been thin, because I heard two men talking. One man with a deep, gruff voice laughed and said that Sabrina Draper needed some Mylanta for her boss, and the other one said he had some for her. The deep-voiced man said, 'Is it doctored?' and the other man said yes. They went on to talk about 'getting even' with Sam Henson. Then the man with the deep voice said, 'You know why Sam pushed Bill Larkin into that Blennoc Project, don't you?' and the other man said, 'To get rid of Sabrina.' But the deep-voiced man said, 'That's what he wants people to think. His real reason is to put Bill Larkin in a position where all that double-dealing Sam's been doing on that project will be blamed on Bill.'"

A concerted gasp rippled through the courtroom. Hannah sat in pale-faced, wide-eyed disbelief. Freddie started to rise but Hannah grasped his arm and pulled him back down.

"Then I couldn't hear them anymore. I went back into the hall and saw the boy coming with a brown paper bag. When he reached me, I took the bag and looked inside. There were two bottles of Mylanta in it. At first, I started to send it back, but I was so angry at Sam Henson for doing Bill Larkin dirty that I took the bottles in and gave them to Sabrina Draper. I thought Sam was her boss and I'd give him a dose of his own medicine," Margie finished and dropped her head.

"Miss Meadows, did you know that the Mylanta had poison in it?"

"I . . . no, sir. I knew something was in it, but I didn't know it was poison, but I wasn't going to allow Sam Henson to harm Bill Larkin, if I could help it," said Margie adamantly.

"Why was that, Miss Meadows? Why did you care about Bill Larkin?"

Margie looked across the room at Hannah and Freddie and then blurted out, "Because Bill Larkin was my son."

Then, like a dam breaking, she stood up and screamed. "I sent Bill the Mylanta that killed him." Margie gulped back tears and swiped her hand across her eyes. "I never got to tell my son that I always loved him. That's why I moved here from Washington. I just had to be near him. He always thought that his mother didn't love him and gave him away. I dreamed of telling him that I didn't want to adopt him out, but my father made me. Oh God! Forgive me," she cried and collapsed.

CHAPTER 27

PANDEMONIUM BROKE OUT IN THE COURT room. Hannah and Freddie tried to get to Margie, but Jerome Judson barred the way.

"Please, Mrs. Larkin and Freddie, just wait. She'll be sent to the hospital. I'll try to get you in to see her there."

Once the medics came in and wheeled Margie away, Keith, whose eye had been on Sam Henson all the time, started toward him. Henson's lawyer was bent over him and whispered something just as Keith drew near.

"Mr. Henson, you seem to have been put in a bad position just now," said Keith, stopping in front of Henson and his lawyer.

"She can't pin a murder on me. Besides, she doesn't know who those men were. She probably just made all that up," blurted Sam, who was then hushed by his lawyer.

Keith's lips set together in a grimace. "Well, we've already learned some things we didn't know today, so who knows what your trial will reveal."

Jerome Judson was in the judge's chambers with the prosecuting attorney. Hannah and Freddie were told to wait where they were. Keith came over to them and Hannah asked, "Why do they want me and Freddie to wait?"

Keith smiled. "Please be patient, Mrs. Larkin. You won't have to wait very long, I don't think."

About twenty minutes later, Jerome Judson and the prosecuting attorney came back in and Jerome wore a smile as he looked at Hannah and Freddie.

The bailiff again called, "All rise." The judge came in, and took his seat, waited until everyone was seated, then shuffled some papers around for a second.

"Due to the unusual confession made by Miss Margie Meadows, the court finds that William Frederick Larkin is freed of all charges. He did not know that anything was wrong with the Mylanta he gave his father, Bill Larkin. The court wishes to apologize for any discomfort Mr. Larkin or his mother has had to endure. The case against William Frederick Larkin is dismissed.

With tears streaming down her cheeks, Hannah looked at the judge and mouthed a "thank you." The judge smiled and turned to the prosecuting attorney. They talked softly before announcing that court was adjourned until nine o'clock Friday morning at which time the case of the State against Sam Henson would be heard.

Hannah was so thankful and needed to share it with someone. She looked at Keith McCauley. He looked across the aisle at her and smiled, then turned to walk toward Freddie with a high-five salute. "See, I told you that you'd soon be out, didn't I?"

"Yes, you did, but I didn't want Margie arrested. She's my grandmother. Did you hear her, Mom? Margie Meadows is Dad's mother. No wonder we both feel so close to her."

Hannah had trouble replying as she fought the threatening tears. "Yes, and if she hadn't given the court that information you would still be in jail. She really gave her life for yours, Freddie."

Keith was now beside Hannah. "Mrs. Larkin, I know you are pleased that your son has been cleared. Maybe you can now begin to recover from all you've been through."

Hannah had been sitting silent but her face was awash with tears. She looked up at Keith. "Yes, of course I'm pleased about Freddie but poor, poor Margie. What will they do to her?"

Keith took her elbow. "Let's go to the car. We can discuss Margie there. " Hannah and Freddie walked beside Keith as they left the courtroom.

Freddie looked around. "What happened to Steve? If we leave he won't have a ride, will he?" Keith explained that Steve had gone in the ambulance that took Margie to the hospital.

Soon they were loaded into the car and Keith sat waiting until everyone was settled. "If you remember, Margie did not know that the Mylanta had poison in it. She knew those men had put something in it but she probably thought it was drugs or liquor. She was just so angry that Sam Henson had done her son wrong that she didn't think. I would have probably reacted in the same way if someone was going to hurt someone I loved."

Hannah felt that she would have also, but still realized that even though Margie didn't know it was poison, she had still done wrong in giving it to Sabrina Draper for her boss, who at that time Margie thought was Sam Henson.

"Won't they still put her in jail, Keith?" asked Freddie who was both relieved and troubled. He loved Margie, who he now knew was truly his grandmother.

Keith started the car. "I don't know what they will do about Margie, but I don't think she'll have to serve time in jail. Why don't we go get something to eat and then see if we can get in to see Margie? I know we can't right now. It's too soon."

"I'm not hungry, but whatever you and Freddie want to do will be all right with me," said Hannah wearily.

"Well, Mom, we may as well since Keith has to take us home and he's going to find out if we can see Margie also," said Freddie. Hannah shrugged her shoulders and nodded in agreement as Keith pulled out.

"What about Shoney's? They have a food bar and you can choose as little or as much as you want. Is that all right, Mrs. Larkin?" asked Keith.

Hannah agreed and then as they rode along, she said, "Sergeant, I wish you would just call me Hannah. You've been such a good friend. I think it will be all right to call me by my first name, don't you think it's all right, Freddie?"

"Sure Mom. I don't see anything wrong with it. Are you afraid someone will talk about you? Surely they won't just because Keith uses your name."

Nothing could have pleased Keith more. "Thank you, Hannah. Now you two are really my friends and friends don't say 'Mr. or Mrs.' when they're talking to each other." Keith looked at Hannah and smiled. Hannah returned his smile just as he pulled into Shoney's.

When they had finished eating, Keith's phone rang. It was Steve telling him that Margie was in a room but was sedated.

"Did he say when we could come to see her?" asked Hannah. Keith said a guard had been posted and nobody would be allowed in or out.

"A guard? Do they think someone will try to harm Margie?"

"When someone has given the kind of testimony Margie gave this morning, it puts them at risk. They also have a guard for Sabrina Draper, but have I already told you that?" asked Keith.

"I don't think you did. Mar . . . I mean Grandmother said that Mom wanted to go see Sabrina Draper," said Freddie.

"Why did you want to see her, Hannah?" Keith asked curiously.

"Well, either you or Steve told us that the doctor wished she had some family. He thought it might bring her out of her coma. I thought talking to her might help."

Keith smiled tenderly. "That's very kind of you, Hannah, but you wouldn't have been allowed in."

"If you knew what I know you wouldn't be so eager to help her," blurted Freddie angrily.

Hannah and Keith both turned to Freddie in amazement. "What do you know, Freddie?" asked Hannah.

Freddie turned red and stammered. "I . . . I just know she is a man chaser and will do anything for money or power."

"How do you know that, Freddie?" asked Keith on the alert.

"I know what Ron Shrader and Nicole Henson have told me, mostly," replied Freddie.

"You mean the Ron Shrader that you go fishing with?" asked Hannah.

"Yes. His dad works in the warehousing part of CEE, and Nicole is Sam Henson's daughter," said Freddie, as if that should settle it.

Keith sat listening to this exchange and hoped Freddie would stop before he dealt Hannah another blow. He soon found a spot where he could intervene when Hannah mentioned that Nicole had spoken to her at Bill's funeral.

"The Henson family, except for Sam, was there, Hannah. The Mitchell family was there also. Did Thomas Mitchell come by and speak to you?" asked Keith. From there the conversation was turned in a better direction as far as he was concerned. He looked at Freddie and realized it was a better direction for him as well.

So, now Hannah and Keith were on a first name basis and Hannah's son was free from all charges. As they rode along, Hannah sat thinking, *God really does know best and He does take care of his children. Thank you, God, for letting me know your love, and now please, please help Margie.* Hannah felt so thankful that she felt tears sting her eyes.

She looked across at Keith. "It seems that unexpected blessings come along just when things look the darkest, doesn't it? Freddie and I have so much to be thankful for, like having you come into our lives, and God has let me know that sometimes things are done through evil intentions that result in a wealth of good for many people."

Hannah smiled at Keith and said, "Keith, we both know that I didn't trust you and didn't like you, but you have proven to be a very good friend. From my heart, I truly thank you."

Keith was almost overcome by the joy her words brought. He reached across and put his hand over hers. "My heart really appreciates that, Hannah. I think we all have a lot to be thankful for, don't you?"

Freddie spoke up from the back seat. "We sure do, me, most of all."

"Freddie, I know you were locked up in a cell, but I was locked up inside. I couldn't see any good in anybody. Without

Sarah and Margie, I think I might have done something desperate," said Hannah softly.

Keith turned a startled face toward her. "Well, I thank God they were there, but we all know that this web will never be untangled unless Margie is freed. She's had to live with so much through her life. As often happens, Margie is one of the Lord's good people and for some reason they sometimes suffer so much."

Hannah nodded her head sadly. "We have to believe it is as Sarah always says, 'The Good Lord is in control' and He will take care of Margie and I hope He helps her soon. I know she must be feeling terrible."

Keith smiled and put his hand over hers. She looked down but didn't pull away as he expected. He was afraid to move, fearing he would spoil this moment, so he tried to be calm as he said, "Yeah, that's exactly what Sarah would say and she'd be right"

Hannah beamed at Keith. "Yes, that is certainly true. I have always believed in a merciful God and I know He will deliver us from the torment of this tangled web of evil, treachery and deceit."

CPSIA information can be obtained at www.ICGtesting.com
Printed in the USA
BVOW07s1726040115

381636BV00001B/4/P